"A cold beer on [...] than sex..."

"Then you're not ha[...] countered with a mi[...]

"Maybe you're right," he said, his gaze unreadable.

Was he going to kiss her? He had that look on his face as if he was going to bend her over and take her right there on the kitchen counter—and if she were being truthful, she wouldn't lift a finger to stop him—but just as he crowded her personal space and she angled her lips to his, his chuckle broke the spell as he deposited his empty bottle in the trash bin behind her.

Drat. Way to get your hopes up, Laci.

"Why, Laci McCall...is that disappointment I see?" he murmured.

"Go wash up," she told him. She didn't want him thinking he had her figured out and twisted around his finger. If anyone was going to get twisted, it was Kane. She'd be sure of that.

"Yes, ma'am," Kane said with an exaggerated drawl that sent arousal coursing through her body. Once he was out of the room, she let out her breath in a whoosh as she sagged against the sink for a minute to regain her bearings.

She'd plainly underestimated the raw, animal attraction still pulsing between her and Kane, even after all these years. Maybe it was stupid to share the same space together, even for a few days. It'd taken her a long time to get over Kane.

Maybe—if her reaction to him was any indication— she never had.

Dear Reader,

Whoa! *The Hottest Ticket in Town* is my first Blaze and I do believe it is smoking! I was a bit nervous jumping into the sexiest line in the Harlequin family, but I think I managed to pull it off, and I hope you agree. The love story between Laci McCall and Kane Dalton is my favorite kind—rekindled first love. I think first loves are the sweetest and the hottest of all kinds because everything is fresh and new.

The challenge is to rekindle that love when life has jaded you. For me—the hopeless romantic— the challenge is part of the journey that makes a rekindled first love...epic.

I hope you enjoy my first Blaze and I assure you, there will be more to come. In fact, Rian Dalton's story is next!

Hearing from readers is a special joy. Please feel free to drop me a line via email through my website at kimberlyvanmeter.com or through snail mail at Kimberly Van Meter, PO BOX 2210, Oakdale, CA 95361.

Kimberly

Kimberly Van Meter

———

The Hottest Ticket in Town

HARLEQUIN® BLAZE™

Recycling programs
for this product may
not exist in your area.

ISBN-13: 978-0-373-79849-0

The Hottest Ticket in Town

Copyright © 2015 by Kimberly Sheetz

Printed in U.S.A.

Kimberly Van Meter wrote her first book at sixteen and finally achieved publication in December 2006. She writes for the Harlequin Superromance, Blaze and Romantic Suspense lines. She and her husband of seventeen years have three children, three cats and always a houseful of friends, family and fun.

Books by Kimberly Van Meter

HARLEQUIN ROMANTIC SUSPENSE

Sworn to Protect
Cold Case Reunion
A Daughter's Perfect Secret
The Sniper
The Agent's Surrender
Moving Target

HARLEQUIN SUPERROMANCE

Family in Paradise

Like One of the Family
Playing the Part
Something to Believe In

The Sinclairs of Alaska

That Reckless Night
A Real Live Hero
A Sinclair Homecoming

To get the inside scoop on Harlequin Blaze and its talented writers, be sure to check out blazeauthors.com.

All backlist available in ebook format.

Visit the Author Profile page at Harlequin.com for more titles

To my Harlequin family...

Twenty-five-plus books in
and I still love calling myself a Harlequin author.
Thanks for taking a chance on me
all those years ago. You changed my life.

1

Laci McCall wasn't raised to cry—not even when it seemed the whole world was falling down…like this very moment.

"Get Laci some lemon water, now!" Trent Blackstone, her manager barked to a roadie when she wavered on her feet for just a blink of an eye. "You feeling good, honey? Sold-out crowd again. Memphis loves you, baby!"

That's right, they were in Memphis. Two days ago, it was Charleston. Next week, it would be Atlanta. A brutal tour schedule was the mark of a successful artist, so she must be on top of the world, right? Yeah, sure. Top of the world.

"You all right, Laci?" Audrey, her makeup artist asked, pausing with her powder brush in midsweep. "You don't look so good."

"Last I checked, you're not a doctor, Audrey," Trent said, gesturing for Audrey to scoot. "She's fine. It's just prestage jitters, ain't it, honey? The minute you hit that stage, you're gonna shine, just like you always do. That's why people come to a Laci McCall show… they all wanna hear that golden angel sing." He looked sharply at the costume designer, who was fiddling with one of the million hand-sewn sequins on Laci's costume and said, "Make sure it's good and tight. The last time, she looked like she was dancing around in a burlap sack it was so loose."

"It's as tight as it's gonna get," Simone retorted, glaring at Trent. "If it were any tighter I'd have to pin it to her skin!"

Laci ignored the back-and-forth between Trent and Simone, secretly grateful that Simone wasn't about to cinch her outfit another millimeter no matter how much Trent threatened to replace her with someone else.

"You sure you're okay, Laci-girl?" Simone asked, worry lines creasing her expression. "I can let it out a hair if it's too tight."

"I'm good," Laci assured her as she tried to take a deep breath but found it difficult. She forced a smile. "It's fine. Beautiful, as always," she assured Simone about the glittering costume that had left Simone's fingers in tatters after hand sewing every single little twinkling piece of hardware onto the fine fabric. "Thank you."

"See? She's fine," Trent said, and Simone, satisfied her masterpiece was going to withstand a full concert, sent a final glare Trent's way and left. Trent didn't like Simone and vice versa, but he recognized her talent, at the very least. Trent returned to Laci with an instant smile. "Honey, you're a vision. There ain't nobody out there in this world that can take the shine off you. That's a fact. Now, get out there and give the people what they crave, darlin'!"

"Yes, sir," Laci murmured with a brief smile as she mentally prepared for a grueling two-hour set. She was just tired. No, she was exhausted. She'd tried to ask Trent to slow the schedule, but every sold-out show seemed to propel him to a more ambitious schedule. Her head pounded with the jarring force of a hammer hitting an anvil, but she gritted her teeth and trained her gaze forward, gearing up for another show. Her people were out there. Her fans made her who she was and she couldn't disappoint them. Without them, she was just a poor Southern girl with impossible dreams and a thirst for something bigger than anyone else in her world.

Buck up, little filly, you got this. The memory of her daddy's voice lifted her spirits and gave her the boost she needed to forget the pain in her head, the exhaustion weighing down her limbs and the fact that her costume did indeed feel pinned onto her skin. Everything was beautiful; everything was right. This was where she belonged and by damn, she would give Memphis the show they'd never forget.

"Hellllloooo, Memphis!" she cried into her microphone headset, her arms stretched wide in welcome. The minute she stepped onto the stage, the crowd swelled with adoration as the resounding chant of her name filled her with momentary joy and she launched into her current number one hit, "You Ain't Goin' Nowhere." Her voice, the one thing about her that made her more than a pretty face, carried the sassy song and for a heartbeat, everything was fine. But then as she hit the high note, belting out her signature raspy growl, the edges of her vision clouded. The stage lights blazed like jet fuel on fire through her brain and the roar of the crowd overwhelmed her eardrums as the sensation that she was falling choked off her voice midset.

Noooooo!

The last thing she heard before she slipped into blissful unawareness was the faint din of complete and utter pandemonium.

KANE DALTON, CO-OWNER of Elite Protection Services, just finished hitting Send on a few important emails when his younger brother, Rian, blew into the office with a perplexed expression. "You're going *where*?" he asked, gesturing to his phone. "Is this an April Fool's thing, 'cause it ain't funny. And if you *are* going where you say you're going, who are you and where is my brother?"

"I see you got my text," Kane said, sighing. "I'm catching a plane to Kentucky in about three hours. I'm just tying up loose ends. You good to hold down the fort for a few weeks?"

"No and hell no. You know I'm not the business guy in this operation—that's your gig. Now, tell me why you're heading to Kentucky, of all places?"

"Warren called. Cora needs some special medical treatment out of state and he doesn't trust anyone else to watch the ranch while he's gone. He said something about not liking the sheriff—calling him a no-good, rotten son of a bitch who'd probably put his own mama in the clink for jaywalking." Rian arched his brow and Kane nodded as he continued, "Yeah, anyway, how could I refuse the guy? He's like a grandfather to us. Besides, you've been telling me to take a vacation for months. Guess I'm cashing that chip in."

"Aw, hell, Kane, I didn't mean hightail it back to the worst place on the planet," he grumbled. "If you look up Woodsville in the dictionary, it's synonymous with hell—not exactly what I'd call a premier vacation spot for either one of us."

"No argument there, but I'm not heading into town. I'm just gonna hold down the ranch, take care of the cattle and make sure no one comes around to mess with things."

"And what am I supposed to do about that job you took on with that senator on his little vote-gathering tour?"

"I guess you'll have to cover for me." He grinned, knowing his brother hated gigs involving pampered, fat politicians who were more often than not leering at young interns and playing into the stereotype rather than doing anything of value with their lives. "Listen, I know it's not supermodels and celebrities, but it's a fairly straightforward gig. Watch the senator's back while he goes on a handshaking, baby-hugging tour and it'll be over before you know it."

"Sounds like a real party," Rian said sourly, then exhaled because he knew there was no getting out of it for either of them. "How's Cora doin'?" he asked with appropriate concern. The old gal was special to both their hearts and even if it had been a while since they'd managed a visit, if she needed something, there was nothing they wouldn't do to make it happen.

Kane didn't have too much in the way of details, but his gut was singing off tune. "Must be pretty bad if Warren's leaving the ranch to take her to this special place. He'd do anything for the old girl."

Rian nodded in grim agreement. "Yeah, true enough. I feel like shit that we didn't see them at Christmas last year."

"Or the year before that," Kane said, suffering a pinch of conscience, but Warren and Cora both knew the business kept them running ragged, which is why Kane knew he had to say yes. Warren never would've asked if it hadn't been the only option.

"Hey, guess who I saw in the news last night," Rian said, switching tracks, his expression turning serious. He didn't wait for Kane to guess. "Laci."

An iron gate swung shut inside his heart and he gave his brother a hard look. "Yeah? And? That matters to me why?"

"Stop acting like a hard-ass. I know you're still carrying a torch for her. Shut up for a minute and I'll tell you what I heard."

"Yeah? So tell me."

"She collapsed onstage last night at a concert in Memphis."

Immediate alarm spiked and his muscles tensed even as he kept very still. "Is she okay?" he asked quietly, not sure he wanted to know. Laci was his Achilles' heel, a weakness he had always done his best to protect by staying far away from her and her world.

"I don't know. TMZ reported she collapsed in the middle of her number one single, and her PR machine is saying she suffered from food poisoning, but I don't buy it."

"Yeah? Why not?"

"Certain circles travel together, you know how that goes. People are saying that she's flat-out exhausted. Have you seen her tour schedule? It's insane."

"Is she okay, or not?" he growled, fighting the impulse to drive straight to Memphis to deliver a fist sandwich to whomever wasn't doing their job and looking out for her.

"Yeah, I'm sure if she gets some rest she'll be okay," Rian answered, watching him with open speculation. Suddenly a knowing smirk curved his lips and Kane swore under his breath. *Here it comes…* "When you gonna admit that you still care for her?"

"When you gonna drop it? We were kids…a long time ago. Neither one of us are kids now. Got it?"

"Yeah, I get it—you're in denial and have been since the day you cut her loose. But whatever. It's your life, bro. I just thought you might like to know."

Kane forced a chuckle, if only to get past the awful pinch in his chest, and said, "Aw, Ri, I never knew you were such a softie at your core."

Rian scowled at Kane's thinly veiled sarcasm and flipped him off. "I hope your plane goes down," he shot over his shoulder as he headed out of the office, leaving Kane to deal with the burden of knowing that Laci was lying in some Memphis hospital bed.

Kane shook his head, hating that time hadn't healed

that particular wound or erased the bone-deep need to feel Laci shuddering in his arms, or hear her breathy sighs in his ear as he took total control of her body. Time was supposed to dull that edge, right? Yeah, so someone ought to let his brain in on that little fact. Maybe if his fantasies didn't feature Laci, he'd get over her. Maybe. But it didn't matter who he was with or even if he was alone, Laci was there.

Irritated at himself, Kane finished his to-do list, then closed up the office to pack for a trip he didn't want to make. Woodsville, Kentucky—home of his miserable childhood and the keeper of his most private dreams. If it hadn't been for summers at the Bradford ranch… he didn't know where he and Rian might've ended up. Probably nowhere good.

Of all the things the Bradford ranch reminded him of—fresh corn bread and hot beans simmering in a cast-iron pot, corn on the cob and steaks big enough to satisfy the appetites of two growing young men—there was only one thing that ever jumped to mind when he thought of those blistering summer days and time hadn't dulled those memories.

Sweet as seasonal rain and with curves for days, there were still times she invaded his dreams, leaving him rock hard, aching and reaching for a woman who was never meant to be his.

Kane physically shook himself from his reverie, appalled at his own mopey melancholy. When did he become such a sap? Apparently, Woodsville brought out the worst in him.

Well, one thing was for certain, no matter where

Laci was…leaving her behind had been the best thing he could've ever done for her—and for himself.

So what if the scar remained tender to the touch. Everyone had scars. Some people just hid them better than others.

2

LACI OPENED BLEARY eyes to blink at her unfamiliar surroundings. *Where was she?* Disoriented, she struggled to sit up and discovered she was lying in a hospital bed and tethered to an IV. *What the...* And just as panic began to cloud her thinking, her memory returned with a flash and she realized she must've collapsed onstage.

Lifting her arm to stare at the plastic tubing delivering who knows what into her vein, she closed her eyes again, still too tired to truly process the ramifications of what'd happened. The lights, the sold-out arena, the total collapse. She should feel guilty but she didn't. Did that make her a bad person? Her thoughts drifted on the tide of her bone-deep exhaustion and she would've sunk into blessed sleep if Trent's voice hadn't jarred her back into awareness.

"There she is." Trent's drawl made her jump and reluctantly open her eyes to focus on her manager as he came into the room with a big, relieved grin. "Thought you were gonna sleep the day away, honey. How you feelin'? That's one helluva way to grab a little R&R, you know. You scared me, girl."

A faint smile found her lips to humor Trent, but honestly, Trent was the last person she wanted to see right now. Of course, that uncharitable thought made her cringe with guilt. Trent was the reason she was on top, making millions and selling out shows. Her daddy had always warned her about biting the hand that was handing out the goods, but right about now she was feeling kind of snappy and she didn't trust her mouth not to say something bad. Trent didn't seem to notice, though.

"Girl, my heart just about fell out of my chest when you collapsed onstage," Trent said, seeming genuinely concerned. "I wish I'd known just how puny you'd been feelin'. Girl, we gotta work on our communication skills," he said, somehow turning it back on her. Hadn't she told Trent a million times that she was exhausted? Maybe she hadn't been entirely clear, she realized, feeling as if she'd not only let down her fans but the man who was making all her dreams possible.

"I'm sorry," she murmured through numb lips. She rubbed at her mouth absently, wondering why the words tasted hollow. She was sorry, she truly was, for making a mess of things, but a part of her couldn't muster the energy to give the emotion much more than lip service and she knew that was just ugly of her. Tears burned beneath her lids as she rubbed her eyes. "I didn't realize just how tired I was, I guess."

"Well, all's well that ends well, I suppose," Trent said, pushing a tendril of hair from her eyes with a tender touch. "Now what's important is getting you back on your cute li'l feet, right?" He didn't wait for her answer. "The docs are pushing all sorts of fluids into you, so you might be a little puffy for tomorrow's show. I'll have Simone give you a little extra room in your costumes, okay, sugar? No worries there."

"Tomorrow?" Distress colored her voice. "What do you mean?"

"Darlin', the show must go on, as they say. Docs have assured me that you're right as rain, all you needed was a good night's rest and so I went ahead and rebooked your canceled show. Get this," he said, excited. "We're even more booked than before. Seems collapsing is good for ticket sales. Who would've thought? Anyway, you just focus on getting some good shut-eye and then we'll get you back on that stage where you belong." *Back onstage?* Laci wanted to scream, but she nodded instead. Trent's stare narrowed at her lackluster response. "Is there a problem?"

I'm not ready to go back onstage. I need a break. Can't you see that? The words bubbled on her tongue and when she opened her mouth, she really thought she was going to push them out, but instead, something lame popped out. "I'm just wore out. I'll be fine by tomorrow night," she promised, and in that moment, she hated herself for being a weak caricature of who she used to be. Where was her spirit? Her fire? Laci McCall didn't used to be such a pushover. Somewhere along the way she'd sacrificed that innate quality for fame and fortune and it felt just as sickening as it sounded in her head. And yet…she continued to nod and assure her manager that all was going to be all right. *Pathetic.*

Trent, mollified, chucked her chin gently the way he would a kid's and smiled. "That's my girl. Rest up, angel, we're back on track tomorrow."

Laci held her weak smile until he left the room, but as soon as the door closed behind him, she dropped the smile like a lead weight. She couldn't take the stage. She just couldn't. Not yet. She needed…hell, she didn't know what she needed anymore. All she did know was that if she didn't get away from Trent and all the trappings of fame, she was going to die.

A tear oozed from the corner of her eye and slid down her cheek.

"You okay?"

The memory of a boy, handsome as sin, with hair too long and a reluctant smile too sweet, invaded her thoughts.

Times were hard, she knew, but she hadn't expected her daddy to drop her off and leave for the summer as he had. During the summer, her daddy logged in the high country to squirrel away cash for the harsh Kentucky winter. This time, he'd dropped her off with Cora and Warren Bradford, an older couple he'd known for a long time and apparently trusted with his only child. But damn it, her daddy needed her and it didn't feel none too good to be left behind with strangers, even if they were nice folk.

The boy, a year older than her at sixteen, climbed the ladder to join her in the hayloft. His blue eyes were something else, almost too pretty for a boy, and when he flipped his dark hair out of his eyes as he dropped beside her, her breath caught. His name was

Kane Dalton—he and his brother, Rian, were ranch hands for the Bradfords—and he set her heart to jammin' like a bluegrass picker with a jug of moonshine.

He wiped at the tear on her cheek. "What's wrong?"

"Nothin'," she lied with a forced smile. "Just missing my daddy, I guess."

"He seems like a good man," Kane said, trying to soften the blow at being left behind. "At least he's doing something to put food on the table. My old man couldn't care less if his kids eat. All he cares about is where he's getting his next drunk, you know?"

She nodded, realizing she was being whiny and selfish. She'd seen the bruises on Kane and Rian, knew that their home life was worse off than they liked anyone to know. Her daddy worked harder than anyone she knew just to keep them afloat and here she was crying like a slapped baby because he'd left her behind. She braved a smile for Kane, which wasn't hard because he created sunshine in her soul, and asked playfully, "Kane Dalton, you always know just what to say. What's your secret?"

The blue of his eyes darkened as he ducked his head briefly before returning to her gaze, nothing boylike in that stare as he answered with an honesty that rang in her soul like crashing bells. "No secret, Laci-girl. Just tellin' it like it is. I would never lie to you, that's the God's honest truth. I never would."

And then he kissed her.

Sweet, simple, perfect.

Laci opened her eyes, still lost in the reminiscence that'd come out of nowhere. The lingering scent of hay and summer heat remained lodged in her nostrils as the memory of her first kiss blazed through her thoughts and occupied every nook and cranny of her mind.

Kane Dalton.

Where are you, country boy?

The sting of loss pricked at her tender heart and she pushed away the feelings that came with the memory of Kane and those sweltering summers spent at the Bradford ranch together. He'd left her behind, up and went into the military without so much as a goodbye or an explanation of why. He couldn't have sent a clearer message than if he'd tattooed it on her face that she was part of his past and definitely not part of his future.

Well, screw him. Why the hell was she thinking about Kane now? There were plenty of years between that heartache and today and she wasn't going to drag herself down with the memory of that pain.

But one thing she did know—as she eased the IV needle from her arm with a wince—she wasn't going to lie around in this bed a minute longer, just waiting for Trent to waltz back in and prop her up onstage again when she wasn't ready to go back. Tossing the tubing aside, she kicked free from the white, sterile bedding and stood on wobbly feet to search out her clothes.

Oh, damn. Laci grimaced when she realized her glittering costume was all she had in the room, but she wasn't going to let that stop her from getting the hell out of Dodge for a while. *Well, it is what it is*, she thought, grabbing her costume and shimmying into it with a groan as it pinched and scratched. Bypassing her heels, she left her room, bold as you please, ignoring the concerned looks and puzzled glances from the nurses' station, and walked right out the door.

3

KANE'S RENTED TRUCK kicked up dirt as he drove the familiar road to the Bradford ranch, breathing in the sweet smell of untamed earth and summer sun as a reluctant smile found his lips. He'd forgotten how good summer smelled in the South. There was something about the way a Kentucky summer reached into the soul and plucked a tune, even if he wasn't open to listening. He hated Woodsville, but he had to admit, Kentucky was in his blood, even if he ran from it every single day of his life.

It was too easy to remember those wretched years as a boy, too young to avoid the beatings and too weak to prevent them, that made the breath catch in his throat and his shoulders tense. Dale Dalton was a rotten son of a bitch with a worse temper, and Kane hoped he was burning in hell for all the terror and misery he'd inflicted on his two sons. Frankly, Kane thought the old man had died too easy—a heart attack was too quick, over in a flash. Kane had been hoping for a slow, lingering cancer to eat Dale from the inside out, but no such luck. The lucky bastard had checked out with a single zap to the electrical system and it was lights out, sayonara.

The Bradford ranch came into view, an older ranch-style home with a generous wraparound porch and views of the green rolling hills and valleys carved by the river that snaked its way through Warren's six-hundred-plus-acre property. Beech trees dotted the countryside and made for picturesque landscape, as well as created blessed shade that was much appreciated when the humidity was hard to escape.

He rolled to a stop in the driveway and walked into the house, calling for Warren or Cora as he went.

Cora, in the kitchen as always, smiled big and welcoming as she ushered him into her frail arms, hugging him as tightly as she was able. "You've lost too much weight," she exclaimed as if she weren't the one looking as if a stiff wind might knock her over. "Just look at you, you're wasting away to nothing. You need to find a good woman who can fatten you up with some good ol'-fashioned home cooking."

"I'm not the one wasting away," he countered, concerned at how small and fragile Cora appeared since the last time he'd seen her two years ago. Sudden tears pricked his eyes and he blinked them back, unprepared for the emotional wallop at seeing Cora so diminished. "What's the doc saying?"

Cora waved away his question and said, "No talk of doctors or medicine. I've had enough of that nonsense. I want to hear about you and Rian. How's that fancy new business going for you? Tell me all about it while I cut up a piece of pie. Peach still your favorite?" She knew it was, the crafty old girl. He nodded and she beamed, pulling a freshly baked peach pie from the oven, where she'd probably hidden it from Warren. "Ice cream?"

"The pie is good for me," he said, not wanting to put Cora into further motion on his account. Slaving away in the kitchen was the last place she needed to be, but he knew from experience that Cora took orders from no one, not even if it was to protect her declining health. He took a dutiful bite under her watchful eye and there was no need to fake a reaction because it was heaven on a fork. "God, Cora, this is the best damn pie I've ever tasted."

She swatted him lightly on the head with a sharp "Watch your mouth," but she smiled as she slid into the chair opposite him. "Glad you like it. Too bad Rian couldn't come with you. I miss him just as much."

"I know, but someone's got to hold down the fort while I'm here," he said regretfully, but after seeing Cora's condition, he wondered if he ought to have Rian meet him there for when Cora and Warren returned from out of state. "Tell me about this special treatment you're gonna have."

Cora, her soft little hands wreathed with faint blue lines, fidgeted as she shrugged. "Warren's got it in his head that it's gonna make a difference, but sometimes you have to accept that when your time is up, it's up. There's grace in that, you know. But he wants me to go, so I will because he's a good man and an even better husband, but I want to spend what time I have left right here on the ranch. I have my vegetable garden and the animals and that's enough for me."

Kane swallowed the sharp lump in his throat that clogged his airway. He'd known Cora and Warren since he was a mangy, starving fifteen-year-old looking for summer work, but they'd become his only family. If something happened to Cora…hell, he just couldn't bear it. He understood Warren's insistence to try anything, even if sounded crazy, if it meant Cora might pull through this medical nightmare. "Pardon my language, Miss Cora, but that's bullshit. Don't be giving up on a cure. If Warren thinks there's a shot, you gotta take it because there's no one on this planet who can make a blue-ribbon-quality peach pie like you, ma'am, and that's the honest truth."

It was more than the pie and Cora knew it, but it made her smile just the same and her smile was worth a million bucks in Kane's opinion. He finished the pie like a good boy, even scraping up the crumbs, just as Warren walked in from the fields, covered in dirt and smelling like a pasture.

Kane rose respectfully and clasped the older man's hand, relieved to find it strong as ever in spite of the fact that he was nearing eighty. "Kane, you're looking good, boy," Warren said, smiling. "Any trouble getting the time off?"

"No trouble, sir. Happy to help."

Warren's proud smile said volumes. "Good, good. It's too bad we leave tonight. It would've been nice to catch up." He stopped and sniffed the air, then spied the pie on the kitchen counter. "Peach pie! Where'd that come from?" His expression went from excited to distressed as he looked to Cora with concern. "You been in here making that pie while I was tending to the chores? Woman! Are you trying to kill yourself before we even get to Florida? The doc said you need to rest before the flight and here you are working yourself to death."

"Oh, hush," Cora said to her husband, shaking her head as if he was being a ninny. "Baking a pie isn't hard, you just throw the stuff in a bowl, mix it up and toss it in the oven. A child could do it. Now stop pestering me and go show Kane what he's supposed to be doing while we're gone and I'll have your slice ready for you when you get back."

Warren looked torn between wanting to chastise her a little more and needing to do exactly what Cora said, but eventually the ticking clock won out as he grumbled, "C'mon, Kane, let's get this done so's we can hit the road. I don't want to chance missing our plane."

"Lead the way," Kane said, casting a short wink at Cora before they headed out. The old girl was still running the roost, no matter what anyone said about her health. If anyone could beat cancer, it was Miss Cora— that much he knew. It was a small but vital comfort to his worried heart as he followed Warren out to the cattle barn.

"I know it was hard for you to drop everything and come, but I wouldn't ask if it weren't important," Warren started once they were clear of the house. "She's not doing so good and I'm not gonna sit by and watch her die without a fight."

"Don't worry about it," Kane said, shifting against

the pinch of guilt for staying away for too long. "I should've been more helpful from the start. Why didn't you tell me that Miss Cora was so bad off?"

"Troubles are private, son. No sense in burdening others with something they can't fix," Warren answered with quiet pride. "Besides, you have your own life to run. How's that going?"

"Good."

Warren grunted, accepting the one-word answer. "You ever hear from Laci?"

"No, sir. Not since we were kids."

"That's too bad. She was a good girl. I seen her on the television the other day. She always did have a pretty voice to go with that pretty face. She calls now and then, but with her schedule, it's hard to break away, being famous and all that."

Kane grunted as if agreeing, but he didn't want to talk about Laci or speculate about her celebrity lifestyle. Warren sensed his discomfort and obliged him by switching tracks, moving to the list of chores that needed to be done to keep the ranch moving while they were gone. It was like riding a bike and, by the time Warren was done, it was dark and time to call it an early night. After a quick supper of cold chicken and freshly baked bread, washed down with cool lemonade, everyone said their goodbyes and the Bradfords hit the road.

When he and Rian had been boys, they'd slept out in the pump house, makeshift guest quarters that couldn't have been more perfect for two teenage boys. Kane had offered to take his old quarters, but Warren wouldn't hear of it and instead offered up the room that'd always been Laci's. Kane scrubbed his hand over his face with a smothered groan. The worn hardwood floor creaked under his feet and memory sprang to life, vibrant as the day it was created.

"Laci, are you sure about this?" he asked. His seventeen-year-old voice broke, his nervousness at being caught only temporarily muted by the intense, overwhelming need to feel Laci against him. The floorboards creaked and it sounded like a four-alarm fire bell, clanging like the dickens, blaring a warning for all to hear that Kane Dalton was up to no good with sweet Laci McCall! He froze, sweat beading his brow as he tensed, preparing to jump out the window if need be, but it was all quiet. In fact, if he strained hard enough, he could hear Warren snoring from behind his closed bedroom door. Kane's heart hammered in his chest and he half feared a heart attack or something the way it was carrying on.

"Get your cute butt over here right now, Kane Dalton," Laci whispered with a giggle. "This is a one-time, limited offer. And if you don't take me up on it, I might just change my mind and leave you in your sorry state."

Kane glanced down at the raging erection bulging his jeans and he swallowed in half embarrassment, half agony. "C'mon, Laci, if we get caught…"

"No one's gonna catch us, you big scaredy-cat." She grinned in the moonlight, more beautiful than ever, and he nearly swallowed his tongue. "Warren and Cora sleep like the dead. Nothing could wake them. Now…are you gonna just stand there looking silly or are you gonna get over here and show me a good time?"

If his cock were in charge, he'd say, *Hell yes!* And

would be vaulting his way to that bed, but he was torn between the fear of being caught and tossed out for violating the Bradfords' trust and giving in to his deepest, most secret desire and banging the hell out of that country cutie! But he and Rian needed this job and he couldn't screw things up by thinking with his dick, right? Hell, who was he kidding? It was more than his dick that was talking. He'd fallen head over heels for this girl and there was no denying it, even if it was the stupidest thing he'd ever gone and done.

"Kane Dalton…don't you hurt my feelin's now," she teased just as she slowly pulled her nightshirt off, revealing two of the most achingly perfect breasts he'd ever had the pleasure of staring at, and just then, he lost all ability to reason, function or otherwise think with anything other than the part of his anatomy that was sucking up all the blood in his body. "Like what you see?"

"Oh, damn, girl," he breathed, forgetting about the squeaky floor and the possible repercussions. Within seconds, his pants were off and he was climbing onto the bed with Laci beneath him. Her blond hair was spread out on the pillow like a halo, and her nipples hardened like twin berries, ripe for the plucking. His eyes nearly crossed with crazy desire and he lost himself for a brief moment in the vision of perfection beneath him. "You're the most beautiful girl I've ever known," he murmured as she threaded her hands through his hair and drew his mouth to hers for a sweet kiss that sent rocket blasts of pleasure straight to his toes.

She broke the kiss and stared into his eyes. "And you're mine, Kane Dalton. Always. You hear me?"

"Yes, ma'am," he agreed, his heart approving. "I'll always be yours." His fervent vow was as true as any, but what the hell did a seventeen-year-old boy know of anything? Still, it didn't stop him from solemnly promising her his soul. "Nothing'll ever change that fact, I promise."

"I love you, Kane…"

"I love you, Laci."

Kane jerked himself from that memory and shook his head as if he could dislodge it, but the whisper-soft pledge remained an echo from his distant past. He sat on the edge of the bed, wondering if he was going to be able to sleep there. Just walking over the threshold had nearly caused his brain to melt with the recollection of what he and Laci had done in this room, in this bed that summer. What would sleeping there every night do to him? Hell, what was he getting so worked up about? It was a damn bed. It was natural to reminisce about your first time. Plenty of women between that memory and now, so stop dwelling.

He kicked off his shoes and undressed, climbing into the bed nude, as he always did, and prepared to fight sleep because he rarely slept well in a bed that wasn't his own, but sooner than he'd imagined, he was out.

4

LACI HADN'T MEANT to end up in Woodsville, but her rented convertible seemed to have a destination in mind from the start because before she knew it, she was entering the town where she'd often spent summers while her daddy was out logging. The town square, quiet and still bathed in twilight, brought an easy smile to her mouth, even though it'd been a dog's age since she'd been back. Everything about Woodsville was steeped in nostalgia—the kind that sucked you in with a powerful current that was impossible to swim against. Woodsville was as charming as a postcard on the surface, but she knew not everyone harbored sweet memories of this place.

Kane's face appeared in her mind's eye and she fought the immediate catch in her chest. Kane Dalton had been her everything—the light in her soul and the fire in her heart—until he'd gone off and joined the Marines, leaving her behind in a red-hot minute as if she'd meant nothing to him. He'd broken her heart in a million pieces and it was safe to say she'd never fully recovered from his abandonment. Well, some might say she'd done all right for herself but they didn't know her private pain, the nights she spent thinking of him, wondering where he went, or if he was all right. For all she knew, he was dead, killed in a war on the other side of the world. Sometimes it was easier that way—thinking he was dead—because then she wouldn't have the option of looking him up just to satisfy some wicked curiosity about things that didn't matter anymore.

She made a point to never ask the Bradfords about Kane and bless their hearts, they seemed to understand and never volunteered anything, either, which was just the way she liked it. Ignorance was better than knowledge sometimes. It was right selfish of her, but she didn't want to know if Kane was happily married off to some other woman, when that woman should've been her. So, yeah, she preferred to know nothing about Kane Dalton.

But as she was driving through Woodsville, the memories were too strong to deny. Her daddy had started dropping her off at the Bradford ranch, with Warren and Cora, when she was about fifteen. Sweet old couple, they were, but she'd been a terrible brat at times because she'd been mad at her daddy for dumping her off with strangers, even if they were nice enough. Still, they'd been good to her. Cora had taught her how to make the best pies in four counties. She even had the blue ribbon from the county fair to prove it. Not that she had much time to bake these days. Trent didn't schedule much downtime. A pinch of guilt followed at the thought of her manager. She probably should've left a note, but then he'd have followed her and, by damn, she needed some downtime or she was going to lose her ever-loving mind and then where would they be?

She needed peace and solitude and the sound of the farm around her. No more lights in her face, people fussing about her everywhere she turned and definitely no Trent booking her for umpteen appearances until she fell over dead from pure exhaustion. *I'll call as soon as I've had a few days to regroup*, she promised herself, if only to assuage the guilt, and it worked because after that moment, Trent completely left her mind, and for that, she was grateful.

Since she was already in Woodsville, Laci knew exactly where she wanted to go. It was way past the appropriate time to reconnect with the Bradfords and now was as good a time as any. She knew without a doubt that they would let her stay for as long as she liked and that was exactly the kind of hospitality she needed right now. Everything in life that had ever made sense could be found at the Bradford ranch.

When she rolled up to the house, she saw the truck parked out front and smiled quizzically. Warren had always been a Ford man, but this truck was a Dodge. Maybe the old guy had switched loyalties over the years. Hopefully, that was the only thing that'd changed. She climbed the stairs and, when she found the front door locked, she searched under the welcome mat for the spare key—*aha!* Some things *don't* change—and quietly unlocked the door.

At two in the morning, she knew Warren and Cora

would be dead asleep—life on the ranch was hard work—so she figured she'd surprise them in the morning. Tiptoeing to what had always been her room, she slipped inside and closed the door, grateful for a bed after hours on the road and way too little sleep. As if a switch were flipped, pure exhaustion returned and extreme fatigue pulled at her eyelids. Everything smelled like home and safety and all she wanted was to put her head on that pillow. Tomorrow, she and Cora could make biscuits and gravy—her favorite—and catch up. But until then…sleep was all she wanted.

Stripping as she went, she climbed beneath the covers and dropped off almost immediately with what she was certain was a smile on her face.

Thank you…this was bliss.

KANE'S MOUTH CLOSED over a tightly budded nipple and sucked the sweet berry, teasing the tiny ridged piece of flesh until the woman writhed and moaned, arching into his arms, offering more of herself for his touch. Her skin was like the smoothest alabaster, perfect in every way. Her breasts overflowed his hands and he squeezed the abundant flesh with a groan as he moved to the other nipple. Her breathy pants fueled his need to touch and feel every inch of her, to know what made her squirm, what made her cry out with abandon. He needed to know everything about her. He wanted to own her cries and make her body quake with each thrust. His finger slid between her slick folds, searching for that sweet heat, testing and teasing. There was something so familiar about the way she cried out, the way she clung to him, pressing herself against him so that every part of her was touching him in some way. Her body, soft and willing, created a carnal need so fierce that his hands shook as he gripped her hips and ground his swollen cock against her. Their tongues collided with urgent, desperate thrusts as they swallowed each other's breath and created a maelstrom of lust and want between them. Good God, his heart hammered with a ferocity that he'd never experienced. He needed that slippery heat as much as he needed air to breathe. He wanted to plunge inside her, going balls deep, straight to the hilt, but as he was poised above her, ready to slide into blessed home, something—an errant sensation, a discordant moment amid total bliss—caused him to realize he wasn't dreaming and that he was about to make love with a complete stranger.

Kane's eyes flew open and he stiffened, ignoring the aching pulse between his legs, as he stared down at the woman beneath him, her arms still looped around his neck with drowsy desire. Her eyelids fluttered open and her mouth opened in confusion, followed by alarm. "Oh my God!" she cried, jerking her arms away from his neck and then pushing at his chest. "Get off me! What the hell do you think you're doing?"

It was then that he realized that he was lying on top of—*son of a bitch!*—Laci McCall.

OH, GOOD LORD! Laci's cheeks burned with mortification as, of all people, Kane Dalton stared down at her with sudden dawning recognition. What the hell was *he* doing in *her* old bed at the Bradford ranch? She pushed at his chest, refusing to appreciate all that solid muscle beneath her fingertips or the fact that he felt pretty good on top of her, glaring as she demanded that he get off. "I don't know what the hell is going on, but if you don't get yourself off me right now, I'm going to turn you from a rooster to a hen in about five seconds."

"No need for that," he bit out, seemingly just as thrown off-kilter by the current events as he rolled off her, taking most of the blankets with him, further exposing her naked body. She gasped and retrieved the blanket, scooting as far away from him as possible. Ten seconds ago, their tongues had been in each other's mouths and he'd been about to…oh, goodness gracious… *Yeah, you know what he was gonna do and you were about to let him!*

She gathered the blankets around her tightly, even though she realized it was a lot like closing the barn door after the horses have already run out, but it gave her some sense of control in a whacked-out situation. Damn, he looked good. He was a breath of fresh air after too much time spent on a tour bus. *Stop that!* Kane had always been a good-looking devil, but that didn't mean he wouldn't lead a girl straight to hell with a smile on his handsome face. "So? Explain yourself," she said, glaring.

"Me? I was asked to take care of the ranch while the Bradfords go to Florida for a special cancer treatment for Cora. How about you? Last I heard, you haven't been around this ranch in close to five years, too busy going off and getting famous and all that to visit. Warren and Cora might make excuses for you, but I sure as hell ain't gonna do it. So that brings me back to my original question… What the hell are you doing here?"

Her mouth dropped open, filled with ready and hot words to defend herself, but there was something else that caught her attention and jerked her around. "Cancer? What do you mean, cancer? Nobody told me Cora was sick," she said, genuinely concerned, forgetting for the moment that she and Kane were still naked in a room together. "How sick?"

"That's not for me to say," Kane answered gruffly. "If Cora wanted you to know, she would've found a way to tell you."

"Don't be a jerk. I have just as much right to know about Cora's illness as you do. She was like family to me and you know it."

"Do I? Do I know that? Because the way I see it, you plain disappeared and walked away from anyone who'd ever meant anything to you, including the Bradfords."

"Shut your mouth. Don't you dare talk to me about walking away when that's exactly what you did when you joined the Marines, leaving me behind as if I were an old sack of potatoes," she retorted, her fury returning in a blaze of fire. "You've some nerve, Kane Dalton, to talk to me like you've got a leg to stand on. You left me without so much as a 'catch you later' and I was left to deal with the fallout."

Kane buttoned his lip—as well he should—and didn't deny her accusation, but that didn't stop him from maintaining his position. "The situation between me and you ain't got nothing to do with the Bradfords. You could've kept in contact and if you had, you would've known about Cora."

"I did keep in contact as much as my schedule allowed," she told him as tears pricked her eyes, but she held them back. He was right. She should've made more of an effort, but Trent kept her moving at breakneck speed and it was hard enough to remember what city she was in, much less to call people from her former life. But she couldn't say that—even to her own ears it sounded petty and self-absorbed, no matter that it was the truth—and so she swallowed her tears and her need to defend herself and simply jerked a short nod, conceding a small point. "I love the Bradfords and they love me. If you don't believe me, you can go screw yourself." Ignoring her nakedness, because who cared at this point, she tossed the blanket away and climbed from the bed, proud as you please, then scooped up her discarded clothing and walked from the room with her head held high. *Take a good look, Kane, because it's the last one you're gonna get!*

5

HOT DAMN, THAT ass was going to be the death of him, Kane thought as Laci left the room, purposefully giving him an eyeful out of spite. Oh yeah, he knew it was spite, too, because he could see it in the angry twitch of her sweet hips as she exited. She'd wanted him to know exactly what he was missing—as if he didn't already know—and make him hurt with the knowledge. His cock throbbed with plaintive disappointment and he pushed at the stiff member with irritation. *Ain't nothing gonna happen with you, so settle down.*

He found his jeans and a T-shirt and went straight to the kitchen for some coffee and a slice of Cora's peach pie. It didn't matter that Laci was here; the chores waited for no one—that was one thing he'd learned all those years ago and nothing had changed that fact.

He found Laci already brewing the coffee, except he noted with a mix of relief and disappointment that she'd dressed—although the short sparkly number wasn't exactly made for modesty—and he wondered what her plans were. She couldn't stay, that was all he knew, but he'd wait until after he'd had his pie to deliver that sour news.

"Did you leave your tiara at home?" he asked, gesturing to her getup with a grimace. "What the hell are you wearing?"

Laci glared. "Don't you dare get after me for what I'm wearing because it's none of your business." She glanced down at the short, impossibly tight dress, but admitted snippily, "If you must know, it's all I had with me. I left in a hurry."

That begged more questions, but he bit his tongue. He didn't want to know what trouble she was in. Whatever was happening in her life was her own doing. Still, he didn't think he could focus with her traipsing around in that sparkly thing. "I'm sure Cora wouldn't mind if you borrowed a dress or shirt or something other than that thing," he said.

"There's no way I'm going to fit into anything Cora can wear and you know it. You're just going to have to deal with me in my costume until I can get to town and pick up some supplies."

"Whoa, now. What are you talking about? You thinking of staying?" The alarm in his voice did nothing for her already prickly disposition, but he couldn't help it. "C'mon now, what are you thinking? Don't you have your famous life to get back to?"

"You hush your mouth before you choke on your damn foot," she snapped with a glower. "I can see right now some things never change. Tact was never your strong suit."

"Don't see no point in sugarcoating shit."

Laci drew a deep breath and started over. "I didn't come here to fight with you. I didn't even know you would be here, but we have ourselves a situation that we need to work together to figure out."

He crossed his arms and waited. "This ought to be good. Tell me how we're going to work this out? I'm all ears."

"So the Bradfords aren't here and you're taking care of the ranch for them," she surmised.

"That's about the long and short of it, but I fail to see how that creates a situation for the two of us when it seems pretty clear to me what the solution is."

Her gaze narrowed. "Is that so? Enlighten me."

"You leave. I stay."

"And why should I have to leave? The Bradfords have extended a standing invitation to me. I have every right to be here with their blessing."

"Why would you want to?" he asked point-blank. "It's not like we're the best of friends. I have a purpose for being here...you don't." She bit her lip, her gaze acknowledging that fact, but there was something else there, something she wasn't saying, that she held back. Kane didn't want to care, but he couldn't seem to help himself, saying roughly, "Listen, you've got your reasons for coming and it's none of my business. All I'm saying is that I can't leave because I made a commitment to the Bradfords. You can stay or go, your choice, but if you choose to stay, it could be awkward."

"So you wouldn't care if I stayed?"

Hell yes, he would care. "No," he lied, because there

was no sense in adding more fuel to the fire. The fact
was, there was some truth to her accusation that he'd
left her behind, but she didn't know the whole story, nor
would he tell her, either—that was his gift to her, even
if she never knew the whole of it. But he supposed if
his arm were twisted, he'd have to admit there was no
harm in letting her hang out if she needed to. The ranch
was plenty big enough. Hell, he could take the pump
house and let her stay in her old bedroom. He exhaled a
long breath, prepared to do the one thing he never saw
himself doing. "We got off on the wrong foot…you can
stay. I'll move out to the pump house and give you the
room. If we stay out of each other's hair, everything
should be fine. We're adults, right?"

"Yeah," she agreed and damn, if that wasn't the right
thing to remind each other at the moment because he
was fairly certain she was remembering what they'd
almost done this morning as *adults*. She cleared her
throat and smiled, gesturing to the coffeepot. "So, how
about we share a pot of coffee and start over? Can we
do that?"

Sure. And maybe she could stop being so damn easy
on the eyes? He cut his gaze away, needing a minute to
school his thoughts before they gave him away. "How
long you thinking of staying?" he asked, needing to
know how long he'd have to suffer the constant barrage
of the past in the form of the present.

"Just a few days, I suspect. That okay?"

He grunted in answer. "Sure. I can handle a few
days." He reached for the pot and poured himself a mug,
then, because he was practically raised by Cora to do

the right thing, he poured Laci a mug as well before moving to the oven where he pulled out the pie. "Grab some plates, will you?" he asked and Laci smiled with delight as she did so.

"Cora made peach pie before she left? That dear old thing is the living embodiment of Betty Crocker and I love her for it," Laci said, accepting a slice from him.

"Yeah, and Warren gave her hell for it, too. She's real sick, Laci. I don't know if that treatment is going to do a bit of good at this point."

"Really?" Laci's expression dimmed as she took a bite, but a smile lifted her mouth as she appreciated Cora's talent for the culinary arts. "I never could match her recipe, no matter how hard I tried. That woman has magic in her fingers when it comes to the kitchen."

"You come pretty damn close," he grudgingly admitted between bites, trying not to think too hard on how natural it felt to sit here with Laci, talking about pie, because it wasn't natural at all. Not in the least. He'd left for a reason and he could tell by the way things had panned out for Laci that his choice had been the smart one. *So don't start romanticizing sharing a slice of pie*, he warned himself. He finished up and brought his plate to the sink where he started to wash up, when Laci joined him and took the plate from him.

"I got this," she said. "You've got chores to do. The least I can do is clean up."

"Thanks," he said, hating how the morning light glinted off the honey strands of her hair, giving her a halo. In all the years and miles he'd put between himself and Laci, he'd never found a woman who came halfway close to the way he'd felt about Laci. There was a reason she was a superstar—she had something special—and he'd known it from the start. *Back away*, he told himself when the urge to touch her cheek became too hard to fight. "I'll be feeding the cattle," he told her, stepping away, needing to put some space between them right this second before he scooped her into his arms and finished what they'd started this morning. Boy, wouldn't that be the most epically bad decision of his life? Yeah, but if he were going to screw up his life and everything he'd built to this point, he might as well go big, right? *Not really*, the voice answered drily. *Keep it in your pants, big boy, and remember what her daddy told you all those years ago...she ain't for you, son.* Ain't that the truth. Kane started for the door but Laci's voice at his back stopped him.

"I'm heading to town to pick up a few things. You need anything?"

He half turned, regarding her with a slow, deliberate gaze. *You naked beneath me and all the time in the world to make up for what I lost a long time ago.* But he couldn't say that. Not in a million years would he, either. So he uttered the one thing he could, "Nope," and then exited the house as if it were on fire.

MAYBE SHE SHOULDN'T STAY. Laci rolled the idea around in her head, weighing the pros and cons of staying a few days in the same house as Kane when stacked up against the very real problem of their long-buried, but obviously very much alive, attraction to one another. Allowing her gaze to roam the familiar kitchen with its worn hardwood floors, she noted the disrepair creeping up and taking over. Rusted hinges on the cupboards, chipped countertops…everywhere she looked she found something that needed a little TLC. It was just Cora and Warren in this old ranch house and Cora, bless her heart, was sick and Warren had his hands full trying to care for her and the ranch without any help. Why hadn't they called her? She would've flown in the best of care for Cora if need be. Round-the-clock care, even.

Laci worried her lip, concerned and feeling out of sorts for being unaware that all this had been happening to two of the nicest people she knew and loved. She could blame Trent for keeping her going 24/7, but the fact was, she'd stayed away because of Kane. The Bradford ranch was so much a part of her memories with Kane that for a while it'd been too painful to go there knowing that Kane was gone.

Of course, in hindsight, that'd been just selfish. Warren and Cora were good folk and they'd been there for her when she'd had no one except her daddy, God rest his soul, and she'd repaid that kindness by relegating them to a few hurried phone calls in between shows. Laci rubbed at the sudden tickle in her nose. She ought to have the kitchen remodeled for Cora. But even as the thought took root, she remembered how particular Cora was about her kitchen and realized she couldn't go and make a big change like that without the old gal's permission. The shock of it alone might send Cora into a tailspin.

Laci leaned against the counter, her gaze finding Kane through the kitchen-sink window. He crossed the yard to the barn where she could hear the cows making their usual morning racket. A smile found her. She'd forgotten how loud those milkers could be.

The first time she'd stayed here, Cora had filled a mug with fresh milk and given it to her with a mile-high stack of flapjacks for breakfast and Laci had never experienced something so good as Cora's cooking coupled with milk straight from the cow. However, at first, Laci had been resistant, pushing away the milk with a polite "No, thank you" because she was mildly lactose intolerant, but Cora just laughed and asked her to try it.

"I'm willing to bet your stomach will tolerate fresh milk just fine," Cora had assured her, but Laci hadn't been too sure. Her daddy had dropped her off with these old folks and now they were trying to kill her, she'd thought. But her daddy had ingrained in her a respect for her elders so, sending a prayer to heaven, she drank the milk and ate the flapjacks. When her stomach didn't immediately rebel, she stared at Cora in confusion, prompting Cora to say, "I was raised on a farm with nothing but fresh milk and there weren't nothing like that 'lactose intolerant' stuff going around. You know why? Because we didn't monkey around with the milk. It came straight to our cups as God intended and you can't tell me that God don't know what he's doin' when it comes to his animals. That stuff you buy in the supermarkets got goodness-only-knows-what inside it and none of the good stuff that was put there in the first place. That's why your body don't mind it."

And after that, Laci never thought twice about drinking raw milk, until Trent came along and tossed it from her travel fridge, saying milk made phlegm and it was bad for her singing career. She hadn't had a glass of milk—raw or otherwise—in years. Laci watched Kane until he disappeared into the barn and then went to the fridge. She found a glass container of milk and smiled. "Might as well make sure it doesn't go to waste," she murmured, pouring what was left into a mug and drinking it down. A sigh of happy nostalgia followed and she simply enjoyed the quiet moment.

Maybe it was weird, but she'd come to really appreciate the small things since she'd hit it big. Most times, she never talked about her childhood to anyone within her inner circle, much less reporters who asked. Her daddy had done a fine-enough job for a single father, but times had been hard and there was no way of prettying up that simple fact. Her time with the Bradfords had been the first stint of stability she'd ever had, similar to Kane and Rian. Not that her daddy had been abusive like the Dalton boys' daddy, God no, but her daddy hadn't always done a good job of providing a sense of home for his only daughter. *Oh, Daddy...I wish you were still here. You'd know how to handle Trent.*

All she'd done was run away from her problem, but it would be right where she left it when she went back. The dissatisfying smack of reality threatened to sour the milk she'd just enjoyed, so she let it go. She'd deal with that later. In the meantime, she was going to find a way to help Cora without stepping on her toes too much. She turned a critical eye to the kitchen. Maybe some new appliances? Surely that wouldn't be overstepping too much. But first…she surveyed her glittering costume with a smirk; she needed to get a few things from town.

6

LACI DROVE INTO WOODSVILLE, sunglasses on, trying as much as possible to blend in, but really, that was a tall order, particularly while wearing the glittery sparkler of a costume that practically screamed, *Hey, look at me!* While that worked well for being onstage, it definitely made her stand out—in a bad way—in a small town where cotton blends were the norm. The last thing she needed was someone to recognize her and Trent to find out prematurely where she was. She knew she had to return at some point—she had a tour to finish—but she wasn't ready to face that world again. Not yet. First things first, she needed to find some different clothes.

Laci walked into the first clothing store she found, a small consignment/thrift store. She cringed at the odd stares coming her way and hustled to the racks to find some simple jean shorts and T-shirts to get her through the next few days. As luck would have it, she actually found quite a few cute outfits and scooped them up before the stares turned into questions she wanted to avoid.

Standing at the checkout, she asked the clerk, "May I use your dressing room to change?"

"Sure, honey," the woman answered, giving Laci a speculative and openly curious look. "That's some outfit you have there."

Laci risked a brief smile. "Costume party," she answered with what she hoped was a believable lie, but she didn't waste time on details and simply disappeared into the changing room with her new-to-her clothing.

The fact was, being a celebrity wasn't quite what she'd thought it was going to be like. All those people wanting a piece of her every night was more than a little unsettling. All she'd ever wanted to do was sing. Now, people wanted more than just her voice, they wanted her damn clothing, too! Once, a woman had practically ripped a piece of her costume off her body, screeching with victory as she'd sprinted away from Security with her prize. Laci had been stunned that someone would want a piece of her sweaty costume and then a little freaked out because what was the woman going to do with it? But Simone had been pissed as hell because she'd spent hours sewing that costume.

At the thought of Simone, Laci almost picked up her cell and gave her a ring, but she couldn't bring herself to do even that—not that she didn't want to worry Simone, but she couldn't take the chance that Trent might be lurking nearby. *Trent's not a bad guy*, her daddy's voice chided her from inside her mind. *He's made you a star and this is a fine howdy-do you've handed him for all his hard work. I raised you better than that, didn't I?*

Laci pursed her lips. *True, Daddy, but Trent's driving me into the ground. I need this. Just a few days, I promise.*

Her next stop was the small, locally owned furniture store, Bleudell's. She walked into the store and went straight to the appliances. Cora wouldn't want something too fancy, but maybe something just slightly better than what she had. Maybe even the same model, only newer, she thought, eyeing the refrigerators.

"Can I help you find something?" The friendly voice at her back caused her to turn with a shy smile, a little afraid of being recognized, particularly by someone who might've known her when she was a kid spending her summers in Woodsville. "That there is a good model, but the best value is in the stainless-steel one."

"It's for a friend and she's a little stuck in her ways, so I want to get something that's close to what she's got," she explained to the woman wearing a polite, retaily smile. "I mean, I'd love to buy her the state-of-the-art appliance if she'd let me, but I don't want to buy something she's going to end up eyeing sidewise, you know?"

"Do I know your friend? Maybe I can help."

She opened her mouth but thought better of it, saying, "No, I don't think so. She keeps to herself. What's the price on this model?"

"That'll set you back about eight hundred dollars," the saleswoman answered. "I can guarantee that's the best price you're gonna find in the surrounding area."

Laci gave the woman a short smile, murmuring, "I'll take it. Can you have it ready by the end of the day?"

"We can deliver it if you like, honey. Where's it going?"

She shook her head, not wanting people gossiping when they found out it was for the Bradford ranch. "I'll have someone pick it up. Can you show me the stoves?"

"That's some friend you have. I wish I had a friend like you who bought me new appliances. Is this by any chance a special fella you're buying for?"

Laci barked a laugh. "Goodness, no, just a friend. About those stoves?" she asked, gently directing the saleswoman with a smile. The woman took the hint and accompanied her to the stoves, where Laci promptly found one that was strikingly similar to Cora's but newer and pulled her credit card. One swipe later, she had a receipt for purchase and a scheduled time for pickup later that evening.

An hour later, Laci had managed to buy everything on her list, including enough groceries for the next few days. It'd been a long time since she'd cooked a home-made meal and she was itching to see if she could still remember the basics. There was a certain level of happiness at the idea of cooking for Kane, even if she knew it was dangerous to indulge in such a fantasy.

Kane had certainly matured into a fine man, not that there'd been any doubt in Laci's mind that he would. Kane was one of those genetically gifted individuals who'd never gone through an awkward phase in his life. From the moment she'd laid eyes on him that hot summer, her fifteen-year-old heart had started thumping like a jackrabbit's foot and she'd about lost her ability to speak the English language. Yeah, he was that hot. Of course, she'd been a bit difficult back then, angry at the world for problems that had nothing to do with the people around her but everything to do with the fact that she felt abandoned and alone.

By the time she returned to the ranch, she came armed with a take-and-bake pizza that she fully intended to use as a little sugar on top of her request to Kane about picking up the appliances. Cora had always said with a wink that the way to a man's heart was through his stomach and Kane seemed to fall in line with that advice because she'd never known the man to turn down a hot meal.

Humming a little experimental tune she'd been playing around with, she walked into the house, carrying the pizza and beer, and then returned to the rental car to get the rest of her bags. By the time Kane returned from outside, covered in sweat and dirt, the pizza was just about ready and the beer was chilled.

"What's going on in here?" he asked, sniffing the air as he wiped the sweat from his brow with his forearm, pinning her with a look that stripped her bare. *Oh, heaven help me...* He smelled like hardworking man with a side of sweaty, break-the-bedsprings sex, and Laci's knees weakened as her mouth dried.

"Smells good," he said, going to the sink and rinsing his face real quick. "You make pizza or something?"

"Or something," she said, scooting away on the pretense of cracking a beer to hand to him, but honestly, she didn't trust herself being within grabbing distance.

Her head wasn't screwed on straight if she was suddenly panting after Kane Dalton after what he'd done to her heart all those years ago. She began to hand him the beer, but then, on a whim, stopped and took a lingering sip before handing it to him. His gaze darkened, but a faint smile lifted his lips and she shivered against the wickedness that flashed in his eyes. *Dangerous game, girl.* Laci cleared her throat and shrugged because it was truly no big deal. "It's nothing fancy, just take-and-bake, but I thought you might be hungry after all those chores."

"You thought right," Kane said, tipping the beer back with an appreciative swig, and Laci wasn't above sneaking another look at those bulging biceps. "Ah, a cold beer on a hot day…that's almost better than sex."

"Then you're not having the right kind of sex," she countered with a mildly teasing grin. Were they flirting? It felt like flirting, which was probably a bad idea.

"Maybe you're right," he said, his gaze unreadable, but his body language was having a full-on conversation with her ovaries. "Pepperoni?"

"With sausage," she answered, her breath catching when he walked toward her. Was he going to kiss her? He had that look on his face as if he was going to bend her over and take her right there on the kitchen counter—and if she were being truthful, she wouldn't lift a finger to stop him. But just as he crowded her personal space and she angled her lips to his, his chuckle broke the spell as he deposited his empty bottle in the trash bin behind her under the sink. *Drat. Way to get your hopes up, Laci. You're just standing in the way of the trash can.*

"Why, Laci McCall…is that disappointment I see?" he murmured, still crowding her. *Hell yes, that's disappointment*, but she sure wasn't going to admit that and gave his chest a firm push with a scowl. He backed away with a deeper chuckle of amusement, his hands up in a mock gesture of surrender. "All right, all right…no need to get prickly. I was just asking."

"Go wash up—you smell worse than a pig rolling around in a mud pit," she told him, which was a complete lie, but she didn't want him thinking he had her figured out and twisted around his finger. If anyone was going to get twisted, it was Kane. She'd be sure of that. "Don't spend all day in there, either. I'm starved," she added on as he walked away.

"Yes, ma'am," Kane said with an exaggerated drawl that sent arousal coursing through her body. Once he was out of the room, she let out her breath in a whoosh as she sagged against the sink for a minute to catch her bearings. She'd plainly underestimated the raw, animal attraction still pulsing between her and Kane, even after all these years. Maybe it was stupid to share the same space together, even for a few days. It'd taken her a long time to get over Kane, although if her reaction to him was any indication, maybe she never had.

7

KANE STEPPED INTO the shower, his thoughts humming at a fine clip. His muscles ached, his head throbbed, but none of that seemed to matter. He wasn't thinking straight—that much was evident by the fact that he wanted nothing more than to lift that cute country skirt and slide his cock so deep into that soft, willing flesh that his hands shook at being denied. Sure, he'd played it cool with Laci, but it'd taken everything in him not to give in to those lips, presented so sweetly for the taking.

Hell, as bad ideas went, messing around with Laci ranked up there with the idea of a four-cylinder truck trying to pull a fifth wheel, but that didn't stop him from picturing Laci's pretty mouth doing pretty dirty things to his cock as he slid the soap over his body. Like a good soldier, his cock rose for duty and he wasn't above palming it with a soft groan. *Laci, Laci, Laci...what the hell are you doing to me?* He shouldn't want her—he'd left for a reason—but knowing that soda was bad didn't stop millions of people from reaching for a bottle of sugary poison. That's what Laci was—sweet, sugary poison.

And damn, if he didn't want a big ol' gulp.

But he was an adult. He could govern himself. Just because he wanted her so badly he couldn't see straight didn't mean he had to give in to that internal pressure. He could be friendly and keep his thoughts in the PG department. Well, he could try anyway. *Keep it together, she's only here for a few days and then it's back to business as usual*, he told himself as he finished.

He toweled off and dressed in clean jeans before heading back to the kitchen, where he found Laci dishing up two slices of pizza and pulling a fresh beer from the fridge. She sure was pretty as a picture, he noted as he slid into the seat at the old dining room table. She'd swept her blond hair up in a messy ponytail so that a few tendrils escaped and curled in the summer heat and he licked his lips, not because the pizza was making his stomach growl but because he desperately wanted to taste the salt on her skin as he ran his mouth along the column of that beautiful neck. Did she still taste like rainbows and whispered promises the way she had at seventeen? *What? Now you're a damn poet? Eat your pizza before you do something stupid.*

Obeying the curt order in his head, he stuffed his mouth with a bite and grunted his approval, choosing to keep his gaze off Laci and on his plate, but as luck would have it, Laci was feeling chatty.

"So tell me what you've been up to all this time," she asked, making conversation as she bit into her own pizza, wiping her mouth with the corner of her hand like a true country girl, more interested in her food than social niceties.

He bit back a laugh at how stupidly sexy he found that. Was everything she did sexy? Pretty much. He took another bite and answered around hot cheese, "Me and Rian own a business together in SoCal."

Her brow went up in interest. "Yeah? What kind of business?"

Kane hesitated, not sure if he wanted to share personal details about his life, but then his mouth was moving before he could stop it. "We own a company called Elite Protection Services. We provide protection details for high-profile clients."

"High-profile? You mean, like celebrities?"

"Yeah, a few. Some politicians, too."

"And what are you protecting them from?"

Kane swigged his beer before answering, "Weirdos."

Laci nodded, murmuring wryly, "I could probably use a service like yours. Sometimes the fans get a little… touchy-feely."

He stopped, eyeing her. "What do you mean?"

She shrugged. "It's probably nothing but overzealous superfans, but sometimes…they scare me. One woman nearly ripped my dress off. Freaked me out."

"Did you prosecute?"

"No, she was running off with a piece of my costume before Security could catch up to her. Somewhere out there is a woman with a handful of my sequined dress." Her mouth lifted in a small, rueful smile. "My costume designer, Simone, nearly had a meltdown when she saw the damage. People don't realize all the work that goes into hand-sewing those costumes."

He chewed a moment, then asked, "You mean that sparkly thing you were wearing earlier? Looked painted on. Hard to imagine it coming off at all."

"It's tight," she agreed. "But it has to be. When I'm onstage the lights are so damn hot that I about sweat off five pounds each set. If the costume isn't tight, it'll come right off and that's not a show I'm willing to put on, if you know what I mean."

He forced a chuckle as his jeans tightened. Yeah, his cock wanted a front-row seat to that particular show. He did his best to shift his nuts without seeming obvious as he suggested the easiest solution to his mind. "Why don't you just buy something off the rack and be done with it? Seems a lot less labor-intensive."

"I would, but Trent says that if you want to be a star, you have to act like a star."

"Trent sounds like an idiot. Who is he?"

Laci cut him a short look. "He's not an idiot, he's my manager and he's pretty damn smart. He's gotten me booked for a sold-out tour, making me a nice payday."

"This the same guy who's responsible for pushing you so hard that you collapsed in Memphis?" Her startled expression told him volumes. Now he'd just outed himself. He shrugged and lifted his beer bottle to his lips. "I heard something about it on the news. Can't seem to switch the channels without news about some celebrity wiping their nose or falling over in a faint—you included."

Laci fell silent. Either she didn't know what to say

or she knew better than to argue a point she couldn't win because he was right, but it gave him no satisfaction to know that some guy was pushing her so hard that her health was second priority to the almighty dollar. He leaned forward, pinning her with his gaze. "Listen, Laci, I don't know the guy—maybe he's a peach and he's getting a bad rap—but my instincts tell me that I've seen his type before and he doesn't care two shits about his clients, only that they make him money. You can do better than that. You need people who care about you, who will protect you from guys like that."

"Well, you don't know what he's done for me," she countered, but with a lot less conviction than before. "He's a smart businessman and a good guy," she insisted with a little more force, as if trying to convince herself.

What was he doing? He needed to keep things superficial. He wasn't her babysitter or her protector. He shook his head, chuckling. "Whatever you have to tell yourself, sugar. It's none of my business." He rose and collected his plate. "Thanks for the pizza. Went down real good. The beer was a nice touch."

"I have a favor to ask," Laci announced, joining him at the sink to wash the plates.

"Yeah? Such as?"

"I bought Cora a few new things for the kitchen. Can you go to Bleudell's and pick them up tonight? They close at seven."

His gaze narrowed. "What do you mean?"

"I mean, I bought some things I felt she needed… nothing big but a new fridge and stove."

"What makes you think Cora wants those things?"

She bristled at his tone. "She'll love it because it's a gift from me, and look around, Kane, someone needs to lend a helping hand around here. Everything is falling apart."

"The Bradfords are prideful people. They aren't gonna like you throwing charity their way."

"It's not charity," she retorted with a scowl. "How can you even suggest that I would feel that way about the Bradfords?"

"Don't get your feathers ruffled, I'm just saying that Cora and Warren are particular. The reason I'm here is because Warren didn't want strangers poking around his ranch. And he certainly isn't going to like the idea of someone coming in and just dumping new appliances on them without their consent."

Laci opened her mouth to protest but then thought better of it. She chewed her bottom lip, distressed. "I just wanted to do something nice for them, considering everything they've been going through," she said.

He couldn't stay mad because he understood her motivation. Hell, he'd been cursing at the old farm equipment and had been half tempted to get a John Deere rep on the phone and start having some new equipment ordered, but he knew Warren would have a fit if he came home to find his beloved, rusty shit gone. "Your heart's in the right place," he told her gruffly. "I just don't know if it's going to go over the way you think it will."

"I made sure they were almost exactly the same, just newer," she said, and he was impressed she'd thought of that.

"Well, maybe it'll be all right," he said, giving in. Her

relieved smile did weird things to his chest. In fact, he suddenly felt all warm and squishy. Either he was having a heart attack or he was going all gooey over the fact that Laci had graced him with one of those killer smiles that'd always done a number on him in the past. Frankly, he'd rather take the heart attack.

"So you'll go to Bleudell's for me?" she asked hopefully, and he nodded, resigned to doing whatever she wanted because she seemed to have strange powers over his ever-loving mind. She shocked him when she leaned in and brushed a tiny kiss across his cheek, grinning like an angel with an agenda that he didn't trust but couldn't quite resist.

"You shouldn't start fires," he warned her in a low tone even as he devoured her with his gaze. Her tiny top gave the barest peek of her navel and it was that tease that made him nearly drop to his knees and bury his face between her thighs. "You might get burned."

"I'm not afraid of a little heat," Laci countered coyly, going from innocent angel to brazen seductress within a glance. "Are you?"

With you? Yes. His arm snaked out to hook her around the waist, drawing her tightly against him. "You sure about that?"

"It was just a kiss," Laci murmured, her gaze fastening on his lips as she slid her tongue along her bottom lip.

"Kisses lead to other things," he reminded her, quickly losing the fight to turn her loose and squelch whatever was happening between them right now. "Don't you remember?"

Her breath caught and he smiled with knowing. Yeah, she remembered just fine. Good. He wanted her to remember. It wasn't fair to be the only one getting burned by the scorching memories between them. "The hayloft," she murmured, her mouth turning up in a sweet, shy smile. "And summer rain…"

Wet and slippery with enough heat between them to evaporate the fat raindrops falling from the sky—yeah, sex in the rain had been hot.

"And the pump house," he reminded her, rewarded with a flash of intense arousal as the memory slammed into him. "The first time I tasted you."

Laci blushed but she nodded, her breath becoming shallow. "I think of that when I—" She stopped herself from continuing.

He wanted to hear her say it. "When you what?" he prompted, his skin on fire as his brain practically *screamed bad-idea-bad-idea-bad-idea*.

"When I touch myself." Her gaze met his, bold and yet shy, and he knew he'd lost the battle of good sense.

"Ohhhh, sweetheart, you shouldn't have told me that," he said with a strained chuckle because now it was on like Donkey Kong and there was no pulling that quarter back from the machine. Their fate was signed, sealed and delivered. Time to pay the postage due.

"And why is that?"

"Because now—" he scooped Laci into his arms, intent on one thing—putting his brand all over that soft, yielding skin of the one woman he'd never been able to forget "—by morning…you ain't gonna be able to walk—and that's a promise."

OH GOD, THIS was actually happening. Not a dream, not a fantasy but actually Kane carrying her to the bedroom to strip her naked and make her change her religion. She ought to make him stop. She had less sense than a goose if she let Kane follow through with his promise but damn, if she wasn't shaking with anticipation, just as anxious as he was to feel skin on skin—screw the consequences.

Hadn't that been her motto since bailing from the hospital? She hadn't been thinking straight since her collapse, so why start now? Particularly when she couldn't stand the thought of not feeling Kane inside her, so, yeah, asking Kane to put her down wasn't going to happen. It'd been eleven years since she'd last seen Kane and an equal number of years since she'd felt him inside her... She wasn't turning back. Not even if it meant she was making the biggest mistake of her life.

8

THE BEDSPRINGS PROTESTED and squealed when Kane tossed Laci to the bed, but she didn't care if the whole world knew what they were up to. She giggled, remembering the last time, as kids, they'd done the dirty right there in that room—not counting the sleepy almost-sex they'd had that morning. "I thought you were going to have a heart attack the last time we did it in here."

"Yeah, visions of Warren kicking my scrawny ass out at the end of a shotgun wasn't really a turn-on," he growled, ripping his shirt from his body and tossing it to the floor.

Her gaze lit up when she saw the ridges of muscle cording his abdomen, narrowing to a trim waist and firm hips, and she wasn't above simply staring and salivating just a little at his male perfection. He popped the top button of his jeans and quickly shucked them from his legs, revealing he'd been going commando after the shower. His cock, thick and ready, sprang from a short nest of dark hair that she remembered very well, and

she couldn't wait to taste him in her mouth again. Of all
the men she'd been with—not that there'd been a long
list—Kane's cock had been the one that she adored the
most. Thick and long, with a spongy mushroom head
that begged for the loving attention of an eager tongue,
just seeing it again instantly made her wet and anxious
to get the show on the road.

"Get over here, Kane Dalton," she demanded with a
smile as he joined her on the bed, her fingers finding
and curling around his ready erection. "You have the
prettiest cock, you know that?" she murmured right
before she pushed him onto his back and then, pausing a moment to pull her own clothes off, she closed
her mouth over him, sucking the thick, fleshy head
into her mouth and gripping the base while she reac-
quainted herself with his scent and taste. His immediate groan fueled her need into a frenzy and she lost
herself to the pleasure of knowing that she still knew
what drove Kane crazy.

KANE CLOSED HIS EYES, his hips straining against Laci's
clever mouth and tongue and he nearly lost his ability to
hold back, but he wasn't about to come in Laci's mouth,
not yet anyway. He wanted to be the one making her
squirm, making her cry out and shake as she came and
if he was going to make that happen, he needed to get
her off him, *right now*.

"Laci, Laci," he said in a raspy moan as he pushed at
her head to make her stop. But the little vixen knew exactly what she was doing and wasn't interested in stopping. Pleasure tightened in a knot around his balls and

he knew the end was imminent if he didn't do something, but he was paralyzed with the overwhelming sensation of total sexual bliss as her hot mouth and nimble fingers worked him into a state of complete mind-shattering need. "S-stop, I'm gonna come!" he tried warning her, but her resultant giggle as she redoubled her efforts told him that was exactly what she wanted. Damn! So much for being the one in the driver's seat!

And then he came, hurtling hot jets of his seed straight down her lovely throat as she sucked him for all he was worth. Dizzying pleasure spun him out, sending him straight into heaven as his cock pulsed with each spurt that she eagerly swallowed until he was shaking and breathing heavy, and so sensitive that even her breath caused him to flinch. "Holy hell, girl" was all he could say after that epic blow job. If he'd been standing, he would've collapsed in a quivering pile of bones.

But there was no rest for the wicked and he was ready to return the favor. Her smug smile was all the motivation he needed to grab her and toss her onto her back, her delighted laughter firing his blood in a way that smacked of more than just a hookup, but he pushed that aside. Right now, he wanted her taste on his tongue. He was going to make her come so hard that her bones melted. And that was a promise.

KANE HAD THE look of a sexual demon, ready to consume her with a single flick of his tongue, and she was ready to submit to whatever his appetite demanded. She shivered as he rained kisses down her trembling belly, pausing as he rimmed her belly button with the tip of his tongue, and then traveled south, teasing her with tiny nips against her hip bone and upper thighs. She was wet with need and desperate to feel him against her, but she already knew he was going to make her come just as she'd done for him. It was tit for tat in this game, but that was Kane's way. *Bring it on, baby!*

"Pretty proud of yourself, aren't you?" he asked in a seductive tone as he lowered himself between her thighs, pushing apart her legs and baring her to his hungry gaze. Was there ever a man who'd made her feel so wanton, so desired, as Kane Dalton? *God no.* Just the simple sweep of his glance made her think of things that would make a hooker blush.

She wanted to feel him inside her, helpless to stop the carnal destruction as it happened. He had the power to devastate her and she was willfully handing him the tools to do so, but she didn't care.

A witty comeback died on her lips as soon as Kane's tongue delved between her folds, just as his finger pushed its way inside her. She groaned and lost herself to the sensation of being penetrated while his tongue manipulated and teased her clit. *Oh, damn, he was good*, she realized as sweat popped along her brow, and her skin became clammy as pressure began to build at a rapid clip. "Wait!" she tried to stop him, just as he'd tried to stop her, but he wasn't listening. If anything, he just pushed her harder, and, within the moment he began strumming her G-spot, beckoning her orgasm with a crooked finger as his tongue sucked and licked that tiny, sensitive nub, she knew she wasn't going to win this battle.

She emitted a groan from deep within her throat and her thighs began to shake. "Ohhhh, K-Kane!" It was all she could manage before everything clenched and exploded inside her as pleasure spiraled out and staked its claim on every nerve ending. *Ohhhh, God...that was... holy hell...not natural!* Her head lolled to the side as she tried to recover from the shattering orgasm, but there would be no recovery time for her as Kane was ready to go, his cock as hard as ever.

He climbed her body, the tip of his cock bouncing against her belly as a grin split his sensual mouth right before he claimed her lips in a searing kiss that smelled of her own musk and sent her arousal level back into the red-hot zone. "You've learned a few things," she managed to gasp before his mouth descended on a nipple. She clutched at his head as he suckled her, losing herself again as time disappeared between them and all that mattered was her and Kane.

He switched to the other breast and gave it equal attention, his guttural moan as he sucked, enough to send her into space. *This man—he had sexy on overdrive— how could any woman be immune to him?* He was her Achilles' heel and always had been. Clutching him to her, she loved the way his back muscles flexed beneath her fingertips as he pressed her into the mattress, the springs groaning beneath their weight. He was poised above her, staring down, his gaze dark and hungry like a predator zeroing in on its next meal, and she was struck by what she saw behind the hunger, beyond the insatiable sexual need—but before she could spend another heartbeat considering the ramifications, Kane was plunging inside her with raw intensity. She gasped as her body struggled to accommodate him, but there was something so satisfying about being filled completely by Kane, knowing that their bodies joined as nature intended, like two puzzle pieces locking together, forever made for one another. She shuddered as he began to move inside her, thrusting hard, hitting that certain spot with unerring accuracy until she was crying out, bucking beneath him as a wildness took over and she was helpless to stop the orgasm coming straight for her without mercy.

Oh God, yes! Kane! His name spilled from her lips as everything spasmed in glorious concert, curling her toes and rattling her womb. She gave in to the sensation without a second of regret. Eye-crossing pleasure blotted out everything but what her body was experiencing and soon enough Kane joined her, shuddering as his thrusts became more frenzied, and then he stiffened and groaned as loudly as she was crying out his name. There were no words for what they'd just experienced, no way to quantify the sensations rioting through her body like fireflies, igniting her nerve endings and sending tingling messages of relaxation and total satiety to her brain. Her bones melted into the mattress as she drifted in the aftermath of bliss and for that one moment, she knew complete and utter happiness.

It wouldn't last—but she'd take what she could get.

BREATHING HARD, HIS heart banging against his breastbone, Kane wasn't quite sure what had just happened. No, that wasn't accurate—he knew but he couldn't believe it. After all his big talk about keeping his distance, he'd given in to his physical urges like a dumb-ass kid who didn't have the good sense to know when to keep his dick in his pants. An expletive formed in his mind but he kept it behind his lips. An exhale escaped as he wondered what the play was now, but Laci was already talking. No surprise there—Laci had always been a chatterbox.

"That was awesome," she said with a happy sigh and he couldn't help but puff up his chest a little bit at her admission—because, hey, he was a male and that was what males did when females handed out sexual compliments—but he knew he ought to set her straight about the situation.

"Laci…"

She turned to him, her honey-blond hair trailing on the pillow, a sweet smile curving her lips. "Yeah?"

He could probably time his watch with how quickly her smile faded once he told her they shouldn't be hooking up like this and, because he'd rather eat his words than watch her smile die, he did exactly that. There'd be plenty of time for disappointing conversations later, right? Likely a whole lifetime. He lifted on his elbow to crane his neck to see the small bedside clock and confirmed what he'd already figured. "Bleudell's is closed. We missed your pickup order."

She shrugged, rolling to her back with another sigh as she stretched like a cat who'd just been pampered. "Oh well," she said, unconcerned. "They'll still be there tomorrow morning. If you don't have time, I can just borrow your truck and get it."

"I'll go get your appliances," he said, adding with

a slight tease, "like you can manhandle an appliance? When was the last time you did anything with your hands aside from grip a microphone?"

She laughed and latched onto his cock, shocking and arousing him at the same time. "Well, I manhandled this just a few minutes ago and I seemed to do a pretty good job of it."

"If you don't let go, you're gonna get round two before you're ready," he warned her with a growl, but Laci wasn't scared of him—never had been—and she knew exactly what she was doing, too, based on the coy look she gave him from beneath those lush lashes. "Laci…"

"Shh," she told him, pushing him back and straddling him. Her wet core fit nicely on his semihard cock and he half wondered if she'd be the death of him. She leaned into him, brushing her lips across his, her little tongue teasing the seam of his mouth with a quick dart, and he surged against her, gently gripping her ass with both hands as he rubbed her hot wetness against his shaft. He ground himself against her, drinking in her tiny gasps and groans, as he used the pressure of his cock against her swollen clit to bring her to another, shuddering end.

"Kane!" She collapsed against him, her weight on top of him an intoxicating sweetness that he couldn't help but drink in like a man dying of thirst. There'd never be anyone but Laci. Everything about her sparked a need inside him that wouldn't die. He pressed a kiss to the top of her head as she recovered, her heartbeat thumping against his chest, and when she finally scooted off his chest and cuddled into his shoulder to fall fast asleep, he didn't have the heart to move her. Dark rings of exhaustion still marred her eyes and she was far thinner than he remembered. Laci had always been curvy in all the right places, with nice pillowy breasts and a perfect, round ass, but he could tell she was being run ragged by whoever was in charge of her schedule. It wasn't his place to say anything more than he had, but it bothered him just the same.

Tomorrow he planned to say more, too…

He tightened his arms around her, allowing his eyelids to flutter shut, as well.

Tomorrow would come soon enough.

9

KANE MADE QUICK work of the chores and then headed into town to pick up the appliances at Bleudell's for Laci. He wasn't sure this was the smartest thing to do, but Laci had seemed anxious to do something nice for the Bradfords, so he was willing to help her out. He knew the Bradfords would never refuse a gift given with a true heart, but he hoped it didn't stress Cora out too much to find her kitchen messed with. People were funny that way. Didn't matter if everything was falling down around their ears, sometimes they wanted things just the way they were, no matter what other people thought.

The drive was easy enough—not too much traffic going to town most days—but the memories that dogged him weren't friendly. Maybe it wasn't fair to blame a place for the shit that had happened to you while you lived there, but Kane couldn't help scowling as he pulled into Bleudell's. No one in this town aside from the Bradfords had lifted a finger to help them when he and Rian had been two skinny, scrawny kids bearing bruises and desperately hoping someone—anyone—would make Dale Dalton stop beating his sons.

Maybe they'd been afraid of the son of a bitch— Dale had been one helluva bastard on his good days— but Kane still held this town responsible for being too afraid to stick up for two little kids who'd had no one to be their champion.

Unlike Laci, he and Rian had been born in Woodsville— native Hedgehogs, if you will—but he felt no affinity for his hometown.

Summers with the Bradfords had been his saving grace. He often wondered how his life might've turned out if Warren hadn't thought to look past the angry, aloof act that Kane had perfected to give him a much-needed job. An angry sixteen-year-old was trouble just waiting to happen.

Unless you put him to work.

Somehow, even though Warren wasn't any kind of self-help guru, his quiet wisdom had told him that anger was an emotion that had to be worked out of the body with physical labor. Nothing worked better to exorcise those demons than good ol'-fashioned hard work. And boy, had Warren put him and Rian to good use. Hauling hay, milking cows—even helping a calf coming into this world—Warren hadn't soft-pedaled his expectations in any way, but he'd paid them pretty well and for the first time in their young lives, they'd felt good about themselves.

Of course, they'd had to hide their money from the old man. They'd learned that the hard way.

"You thought you were real smart, didn't you? You thought I wouldn't hear that you're getting paid by old man Bradford," Dale had snarled, gripping Kane's collar and jerking him around. Kane had been working for Warren for a month and had saved all of his earnings—three hundred and fifteen dollars—and was planning on buying some much-needed clothes for him and Rian for school. Dale's breath smelled of whiskey and rancid tomatoes, two things Kane had a hard time stomaching to this day, and the mean glint in his eye was hazed from too many days spent drinking too much and eating too little. Kane knew there was no avoiding the beating that would follow if he didn't cough up some cash, and so he gave Dale all but a hundred bucks of his stash, lying to his dad about how much he was being paid. Dale, too drunk to do the math, just took the money and finished his bender but not before clocking Kane just because he didn't like "the look" on his "shit-eatin'" face.

Aw, let's stop with the memory lane, he told himself, rubbing the bristle on his jaw. *The old man is dead. Be thankful for small graces.*

He stepped outside the truck and he saw Warren in his memory, walking out of the hardware store next door to Bleudell's, and he couldn't help remembering that fateful day.

"Got yourself quite the shiner, young man," Warren had remarked, gesturing to Kane's black eye. "Hopefully, you gave the other guy worse."

He was tempted to snarl at the man, to tell him to go screw himself, because he was angry and embarrassed and by that point, everyone had a low opinion of the

Dalton boys anyway, but for some reason, he swallowed the hot retort. Instead, he muttered, "I wish, sir," and started to walk away.

He'd been planning on dropping by the Dumpster behind Olive's Diner to see if there was anything worth salvaging. He'd learned real quick that restaurants threw away a shit-ton of food and for a starving kid, throwing away good food just seemed crazy. He'd found all sorts of stuff that would fill his and Rian's bellies, but he had to do it on the sly because he didn't relish anyone catching him digging through the trash.

But everything changed that day. It was as if Warren had somehow known that Kane was at a crossroads and he had the power to do something about helping him make the right choice. "You look plenty strong," he said to Kane's back, causing him to turn with suspicion.

"Yeah? What of it?"

"Are you honest?" Warren asked bluntly and Kane nodded, not quite sure what to think of the sturdy old guy in his ranch boots crusted with God-knew-what and his dusty jeans, but he sensed that he wasn't out to screw him over or ask him to suck his dick, and he took a wait-and-see attitude. The man nodded as if he approved and said, "Good. I need someone strong and honest for summer work. You available? Pay is decent for the right person."

"What do I have to do?" he asked, wary.

"Just hard work on a ranch, son. Probably the hardest work you've ever done, but I've got a place for you to sleep and three squares made by the best little woman in the kitchen."

That sounded like a dream come true. Hard work never scared him none. Hell, he worked hard every day just to survive. When he wasn't dodging his dad's fists, he was scrounging for food and supplies to keep him and his brother alive. "I've got a brother," he said, knowing that Rian would never survive without him and there was no way he was leaving his little brother behind. "He's a hard worker, too."

"How old?"

"Thirteen, sir."

"Strong like you?"

"Yes, sir."

The man gave it some thought and then shrugged. "All right. We'll see. Name's Warren Bradford. What's yours?"

"Kane," he answered, hesitating to reveal his last name. Dale Dalton was good for nothing in this town and everyone knew it. He sure as hell didn't want to lose out on a great opportunity just because of his dick-head old man.

"Kane…you got a last name?"

"I do."

"Spit it out, son."

His mouth clamped shut, resisting, but he knew there was no help for it and answered glumly, "Dalton, sir."

"That's what I thought. Listen here, son…I don't make a habit of judging people based on the individuals they have the misfortune of being related to. You hear me? You make your reputation with me based on your actions. Act like a solid young man with good character and I'll treat you as such. Steal from me and I'll treat you like the no-good trash your father is. We clear?"

Kane nodded. He liked this old man. There was something true and honest about him that he wasn't used to. "When do you need us?"

"What are you doing right now?"

"Nothin' much," he answered, but his stomach growled and the old man didn't miss it.

"How about we seal the deal like our granddaddies did over a good meal? Sound good?" Kane wiped away the sweat from the summer sun baking his head and all he could manage was a nod, suddenly hungrier than he'd ever been in his life. Satisfied, Warren nodded. "Good. Where's your brother?"

"Waiting for me at Bridgerton Park," he answered dutifully.

"You need to talk with your pop or anything?"

Hell no. Kane would rather shoot himself in the foot with a nail gun than tell his old man that he was getting a job. "No, sir. He don't care what we do as long as we stay out of his way," he told Warren.

"All right, then. Meet me at the park in ten minutes."

And then Warren climbed into his truck and rumbled off, presumably to finish his errands, and Kane split for the park at breakneck speed.

Yeah, that was the day things had changed.

Thank God.

He'd do anything for the Bradfords. Anything at all.

They'd saved his sorry life and he'd spend the rest of his life looking out for them if they'd let him, so he understood Laci's desire to do something nice for them.

He walked into Bleudell's and went straight to the pickup counter. "I'm here to pick up order number W34986, a stove and a refrigerator."

The older, blue-haired woman behind the counter adjusted her glasses and then smiled when she saw Kane. "My, aren't you a tall bucket of water. Now, honey, what did you say that order number was?"

He repeated the number and she adjusted her glasses before bending over a ledger to scan with her wrinkled fingertip. "Aha!" she exclaimed. "There it is. Now, there's no name on here…where is this going?"

"I'm just doing a friend a favor," he answered, remembering Laci's warning about letting people know it was going to the Bradford ranch. The last thing he wanted was to end up stirring the gossip pot while he was here. He left the woman wondering and said, "I'll bring the truck around."

Plainly disappointed, the old lady shuffled away to bark orders at the warehouse workers and Kane walked out, already getting twitchy, and he'd only been in town for fifteen minutes.

Good times.

10

LACI FOUGHT AGAINST her own indecision as she stared at her cell phone. She'd powered it down the moment she'd left the hospital because there was no one she wanted to talk to, but even more so, she wasn't about to take the chance that someone might talk her into coming back. Being off the grid felt good—like the guilty pleasure of eating her favorite ice cream behind Trent's back. She frowned at her own thoughts. Trent wasn't a bad guy—he was focused. And she needed that in her life. There were always sacrifices to be made when going after a dream as big as hers, right?

Maybe it was time to let someone know where she was before Trent put out an all-points bulletin for her whereabouts. Talk about embarrassing. She certainly didn't want that. Laci sighed as she powered her phone on, not surprised when there were twenty voice messages and hundreds of texts. The weight and responsibility of her role in so many people's lives threatened to suffocate her. She stared resentfully at the electronic tether and was overwhelmed by the notion that she ought to just chuck it into the creek and let the world forget about Laci McCall. But that wasn't actually feasible— nor could she really follow through with such a drastic decision. Trent would land on his feet—as he was fond of reminding her, there were plenty of young singers who'd love to work with him—but what about Simone and Audrey? They were part of her team and they worked their fingers off for her. Audrey was a single mom and Simone was helping pay for her grandmother's care in a nursing home. Losing a steady gig like Laci McCall's would be a major blow to them both. She couldn't let them down. She would go back…she would return to the hectic lifestyle. But she needed a few more days.

Was that bad? A few more days with Kane?

Yeah, that was probably worse than she realized. She shouldn't stay here at the ranch with him here. A hotel room would've been safer. Kane had offered to stay in the pump house but they both knew that wasn't going to happen. He was going to sleep beside her every night until she chose to leave. They'd already crossed the line—no sense in trying to put that genie back in its bottle. They were so good together, it was a mystery how they'd ever broken apart.

Well, not entirely a mystery. Kane had stomped on her heart and then walked away. If there was anything she hated more, it was reliving that day because it still had the power to double her over.

"What do you mean you joined the Marines?" she'd asked, stricken. "I don't understand. You know I'm going to Nashville this month. You said you were coming with me." Kane had never looked at her with such distance in his eyes, but that day he was a million miles away and she was as insignificant as a fly buzzing around his head, more of an annoyance than anything truly distressing. She reached out to him, trying to grasp his hand, but he pulled away. "Kane?" Her voice broke as tears started to stream down her face. "What's going on?"

He turned his gaze away from her, away from her tears, with a shrug. "Listen, I don't want to hurt your feelings but your dream was never mine. I just told you what you wanted to hear at the time, but I've got to start thinking about what's right for me, too."

"I don't believe you," she cried, shaking her head. "You said I had what it took to go places and you'd be there with me every step of the way. What changed?"

"Yeah, I did say that, but that got me to thinking. What's in it for me? What am I supposed to do, Laci? Follow you around the globe while you're off being famous? Am I supposed to carry your bags and trail a few steps behind you while the world gets the best of you? I gotta be honest with you…that's not my gig. It never was and I never should've pretended that it could be. I'm sorry."

"You said you loved me," she said bitterly. "I guess that was a lie, too?"

Something passed over Kane's features that almost gave her hope but then it was gone, replaced by the hard light in his eyes skewering her with his decision. "Whatever we had was kid stuff, Laci. You're practically a baby. What do you know about life and what you want out of it?"

"You're only a year older than me so don't act like you're some wise old man," she retorted, her temper returning. "You're just a coward. That's all you are, Kane Dalton—a scared little boy who'd rather run than deal with the possibility that things are going to change. I never asked you to be the guy who walked ten steps behind me—I asked you to be the man who walks beside me. There's a difference."

"Not to me," he maintained stubbornly. "Not in the lifestyle you're choosing. I'm not cut out for that shit. As for being only a year older—maybe so—but I've lived more in my years, suffered more than you can imagine, and sometimes I feel hundreds of years older than you."

She drew back, stung. "You're holding against me the fact that my father isn't a drunk asshole who beat me?"

"No. But our experiences are different and sometimes I get tired of your naive way of thinking when it comes to life in general."

"Oh! Is that so? Well, screw you, then, Kane. Screw you!"

He exhaled, shoving a hand through his hair, as if searching for a better way to drop a bomb on someone but realized there was no easy way to destroy someone's life, and simply said, "Sorry. I did what was best for me. For what it's worth, I do think you're talented and I know you're going to be a star someday. You're just not going to be the star in my universe. Good luck, Laci."

"Don't you dare tell me good luck like that."

"Like what?"

"Like you care."

He made a noise of exasperation as he hooked his thumbs into his belt loops. "I do care, Laci. I just can't do what you're wanting me to and I figured it was best to end it now before it got real messy."

"You could've been honest with me from the start," she said, wiping her eyes. "You never should've encouraged me or told me that I could sing when you never planned to support me all the way. You're bailing on me when I need you the most."

"I'm not bailing on you," he said, quietly disagreeing, which baffled her. He shocked her by pulling her to him and brushing the sweetest of goodbye kisses across her lips. She softened a little automatically because Kane always had that effect on her, but her heart was breaking. He was really doing this—leaving her. "That voice of yours…it's the real deal," he murmured. "Just like you are. Take care, Laci."

And then he released her, walking away. When he drove away that day, he'd actually been packed and ready to report for boot camp. From what she'd learned from the Bradfords, he'd been shipped out the next day. She'd cried for days. If it hadn't been for her daddy keeping her on track, she never would've made it to that audition in Nashville nor attracted the attention of the right people at the right time.

The rest, as they say, was history.

But now that Kane was back in her life—if even temporarily—all sorts of unresolved feelings were bubbling to the surface and she didn't know whether it was wise to give them a closer look or put a lid on them.

She didn't quite know what to do, actually. Her heart desperately wanted to spend as much time as possible with Kane, to pretend that the outside world didn't exist beyond the property lines of the Bradford ranch. Being here made it possible to daydream about the life she hadn't chosen—a simpler life with family and the mundane stress of most people. Closing her eyes, a half smile lifted her mouth as she pretended for a minute that she and Kane had been graced with their fairy-tale ending and that they lived on a ranch like this one, their kids running in and out of the house making a huge racket while Kane did his thing outside and she tended to the kitchen details. Yeah, it was Mayberry, USA in her mind and that's exactly how she liked it, even if it was a total fantasy. Life wasn't that rosy. Sighing, she opened her eyes and knew it was time to figure out lunch. Kane would be home soon with the appliances.

Home.

If only.

KANE FOUND LACI out on the back porch, strumming her guitar and testing out a new tune. He stopped, transfixed by the sight of her sitting there, feet tucked under her in the old wicker chair, her guitar across her chest, her hair tied up in a messy knot by a red bandanna. The sunlight bathed Laci in a warm yellow glow, lighting up the highlights in her hair like something out of a shampoo commercial, and he could do nothing but stare with hungry eyes.

God, was there ever a more beautiful woman on this planet than Laci McCall? Not in his world. Laci had won the genetic lottery, blessed with looks and talent, and brains, too.

And, *hot damn!*, that girl was sexy. As if sensing he was there, she looked up and smiled, brightening his day with that guileless sweetness that was inherently Laci. Within that one look, he forgot all about everything that rubbed him the wrong way and he returned the smile.

"What you working on?" he asked, climbing the porch to join her.

"Just something that keeps popping into my head," she answered, adding bashfully, "It's not done yet. Not even a little."

"Can I hear it?"

"You want to?"

"Of course," he said, settling into the opposite wicker chair.

"What about the appliances?"

"They aren't going nowhere. They can wait a minute while I listen to your song. Unless you don't want to…"

"No, no," she rushed to assure him with a quick smile, bending to pluck at the strings to get her bearings. She settled and then began, strumming her guitar as her sweet voice brought the lyrics to life.

"Someday time will belong to me, someday you'll come to me but someday ain't here just yet so I wait by that place we always knew…that place where we were true."

She finished the chord and Kane had to work to swallow the sudden lump in his throat. Was she talking about their past? Did she feel that way about him still? So much water under that bridge.

She peered at him almost shyly. "Well? Did you like it?"

"It's good," he admitted, clearing his throat of the emotion stuck in it. "Sounds like another hit."

"Maybe if I could finish it," she retorted, setting her guitar beside the chair. "It's been stuck in my head for weeks. I can't seem to find the rest of the song. Just when I think I've got it, it jumps out of reach."

"You'll get it."

"You think so?"

"I do," he answered with a solemn nod. Laci was the real deal, not a flash in the pan, a one-hit wonder. He may not be sure of many things but he was sure of that one fact. "Just keep trying." He wanted to ask if the song was about them but the words wouldn't come. Maybe he was afraid to find out that she was singing about someone else. Or maybe he was equally afraid that the song *was* about them. He popped from the chair with a forced smile. "You ready to help me get these appliances in?" he asked.

"Sure," she said, grabbing the neck of her guitar. "Let me just put this away first. I'll meet you at the truck."

He nodded and strode away, his thoughts warring with the sudden ache in his heart. They never should've had sex. Now his head was a jumbled mess and he didn't know which end was up anymore. Before he'd left Los Angeles, he'd known his purpose, his mind and his heart. Now? He didn't have a clue. All he wanted was

Laci. Laci—all day, every day. It was as if there was a Laci channel in his brain and his remote was broken.

And that was bad news—for him.

Because the bottom line was…Laci was a superstar and there was no room in her life for someone like him.

Just as there'd been no room for him all those years ago.

Remember that.

Yeah, yeah, how could he ever forget? It was the day his heart broke—and never recovered.

11

"I NEED A FAVOR," Trent said to his friend Wes Borchard as he toyed with the sodden napkin beneath his sweating glass. He hated asking for these types of favors, but he was never one to shirk from unpleasant tasks. "A favor that only someone with your connections can provide, if you catch my meaning."

Wes barked a laugh, eyeing him with speculation. "Such as?"

"It's nothing too terribly invasive...you might've heard of my client Laci McCall?"

"The hot singer, the blonde?"

"That's the one. She's burning up the charts and selling out concerts. Have you ever been to one of her shows?"

"Can't say that I have."

"You're missing out, friend," Trent said amiably, but he could see that Wes wasn't impressed by his celebrity client and returned to the point. "Here's the thing, Wes...she's missing."

That made Wes pay more attention. "Have you reported her missing? Why are you telling me instead of the authorities?"

"Calm down, Wes, I doubt she's been abducted or anything like that. The fact is, I've been pushing her pretty hard and I think she just needed a little breathing room, which honestly, if we didn't have a sold-out gig scheduled for this Friday, I wouldn't care. But that's not the case—I need her back. And that's where you come in."

"You want me to trace her credit card transactions," he surmised, relaxing a little, but keeping his gaze sharp. "That's illegal, Trent. You know that. American citizens have rights."

"Yeah, and I have cold, hard cash. Name your price and it's a done deal."

Wes shook his head, smiling. "You've got some iron balls, Trent. Iron balls. I could lose my job for something like this. What then?"

"Only if you get caught and it's really such a small thing."

"Too risky."

"Since when?" Trent had used Wes's talents in the past, but suddenly *now* he gets cold feet? Great timing to grow a conscience. He tried a different approach. "I hear you. How about this…maybe she's in danger…*maybe* I'm wrong and I should've reported her disappearance to the authorities, but given her celebrity status…I really don't want the media to get a hold of this if it's not necessary, you understand?"

"I suppose if you thought there might be a threat, I could do some checking around…"

"See? Exactly. You'd really just be checking on the safety of a young woman who has had more than a few death threats. That's the truth," he told Wes with a shrug. "I mean, I had them checked out and the threats were baseless, but you never know where the true crazies are hiding."

"Sometimes in plain sight," Wes supplied with a faintly mocking smile. "Why'd she run away from you?"

"She's a spoiled princess who doesn't want to finish the job she started," Trent said, waving away Wes's insinuation. "She's talented enough and nice enough to look at, but she's a handful. It's a full-time job keeping her on track."

Wes exhaled and lifted his hands. "I can't take a bribe." Trent nearly swore at the stupid game Wes was insisting on playing—as if the man had such a straight moral compass! "I'd like to help but…"

"Of course not. I completely understand." Trent smiled briefly, cutting his gaze around the small outdoor café. "So what's new with you? Anything you're working on?"

"Actually, yes, thanks for asking. The wife and I are building an addition to our home, but man, those contractors…greedy bastards. Every time I turn around, a new bill higher than the last lands on my desk. I wish I could do *something* about that."

Ah, there's your currency. Trent brightened. "You're in luck. I happen to know a really good contractor…

one who might be able to help you with your situation. Would you like his number?"

"Would you mind? That would be great."

"Sure, sure. Here, let me write down his number for you." He jotted down Laci's personal information and slid it to Wes. "You give him a call and let him know that I sent you. He'll see that you're done up right and if you have any problems, don't hesitate to give me a call and I'll take care of it." *As in, I'll pay the bill.* Good grief, this information was going to cost him. His mouth curved in a short-lived smile. "That work for you?"

"Absolutely." He pocketed the card with Laci's information. "You're a good *friend.* I'll be in touch."

Trent jerked a nod and then he rose. "I look forward to your call."

Wes did a mock salute and laughed as Trent, sliding on his Wayfarers, walked out of the café.

LACI WATCHED WITH a half smile on her lips as Kane finished rubbing down the horses and then tossed them some hay. He hadn't seen her yet. It was hot in the barn. The air smelled of hay, summer sun and horses—frankly, the intoxicating scent was more of an aphrodisiac than any oyster on the half shell could hope to be. The day had gone by quickly. They'd managed to get the new appliances installed and going and Kane was planning to take the old ones to Goodwill the following morning. She had a roast in the Crock-Pot and she'd come out to tell him it was time to eat, but she'd caught him talking to Jasper, one of the oldest horses in the stable, one that Kane himself had learned how to ride from. His touch was gentle, his voice low…and Laci was moved by the amount of love that still remained between man and horse even after so much time had passed. *You shouldn't be horning in on a private moment—it has nothing to do with you*, a voice chastised her, and she reluctantly cleared her throat. Kane glanced up and even though that sensual mouth didn't lift in a smile, she saw the way his eyes lit up when he realized it was her. A funny tremor tickled her belly and she entered the barn. "Dinner is almost ready. I thought you might want to get washed up."

"I'm just about finished here," he said, returning to Jasper and rubbing him affectionately on the nose. "Can't believe the old man is still around."

"Horses live to be pretty old," she said, smiling as she rubbed Jasper's neck while he crunched the alfalfa. "He's still beautiful as ever."

"He's a good-looking boy," Kane agreed, stepping away from the stall and going to check on the other two horses, Amelia and Dancer. "You go on ahead, I'll be in, in just a minute."

"I don't mind waiting," she murmured. The truth was, the memories of their time in this barn were something of a powerful force. It was too easy to remember what they'd done to each other in the hayloft, too easy to crave doing it again. She probably shouldn't but… "You remember the last time we were in here together?"

He paused and cut her a quick look. "Laci…"

"You remember."

Kane fell silent before agreeing quietly, "Of course I remember. That's not something a man forgets."

"Good." And then she made an impulsive decision, suddenly pulling her sundress up and over her head, standing there in her bra and panties with a bold smile. *What do you think about that, Kane Dalton?* His groan told her exactly what he thought and it tickled her pink. Or more specifically, it tickled her pink parts. She giggled and beckoned as she climbed up into the hayloft. "Come and get it, baby. Let's re-create history."

Aw, HELL. *He was only human!*

Kane's mouth dried, his cock sprang to attention and his brain practically stalled as all systems just went on high sexual alert. Before he knew it, he was climbing that ladder because damn, if he was going to have the willpower to walk out that barn with Laci half-dressed waiting for him to do terrible things to her.

He found her lying on the hay, smiling like a dirty little angel, and he nearly busted a nut right there. *Get a hold of yourself, Dalton. Don't go embarrassing yourself.* He pulled his shirt up over his head and tossed it, unbuttoning his jeans as he went. She started to shimmy out of her panties, but he stopped her with a growl. "Let me," he told her, pulling the tiny straps at her hips down, revealing that sweet pussy with its strawberry-blond curls. "Damn, girl," he breathed, gazing down at her with the raging sexual hunger of a man who hadn't felt a woman beneath him in too long when, in fact, they'd had sex just last night. But it'd always been this way with them—insatiable.

"Remember what you did to me," she asked in a

small, teasing voice, biting her lip. "The first time you'd ever…"

"Went down on someone," he finished for her in a tight voice. "Yeah, I remember. You were my first for a lot of things."

"Got any more tricks up your sleeve?" she asked with warm, sultry approval.

"Maybe." He grinned.

She practically purred as she said, "Show me, baby. Show me what you can do to me."

"With pleasure," he said, wasting no time in going to the floor to gather her in his arms, drawing her legs up over his shoulders so that her sweetly feminine pussy was right under his nose. He inhaled deeply, loving her unique scent, then plunged his tongue between those folds, drinking in her gasps and moans, taking great care to listen to her subtle cues. When she thrashed, he pulled back, giving her time to recover but not enough time to allow her arousal to fade, then he slipped his finger inside her and tickled her G-spot, impaling her on his finger as his tongue swirled and sucked that tiny, responsive nub until she was crying out his name in tortured gasps.

"God, yes, Kane!" She shuddered and sobbed as he sucked the orgasm right out of her, licking her juices and enjoying every subtle taste and nuance of her arousal. It was like the finest wine and hers was the only label he'd acquired a taste for.

"Kane, Kane, Kane," she said softly, repeating his name like a prayer as she rocked against the waves of pleasure still buffeting her. Her pussy clenched around his finger and he pressed her G-spot, smiling with satisfaction when she shuddered again with a moan. He could make her come again but he wanted to be inside her when she came this time.

He withdrew his finger and popped it into his mouth, grinning when she blushed, but soon enough his cock was in her mouth, and she was sucking and licking, determined to send him over the edge just as she had before, but this time he had more control and he gently pulled away. "Not so fast, you little heathen," he growled, turning her so that her back was to him. He reached around to pinch her nipples while nibbling her neck. Her pert, rounded ass pressed against him and his cock fit perfectly against the cleft. Leaving her breasts, he took his cock in hand and began sliding it against her flesh, teasing her with the head, causing her to gasp and push against him. "You want that cock, sweet girl?"

"You know I do," she answered, rolling to her back. "Are you going to tease me or actually give me what I want?"

"Spoiled rotten," he said with a beleaguered sigh that wrenched a laugh out of her as she looped her arms around his neck to pull him to her. "You shouldn't always get what you want…you'll become unbearable."

"Just try to tell me no and see what happens," she warned playfully before sealing her mouth to his, instantly deepening the kiss between them as the heat leveled up. Everywhere hands and mouth touched and kissed ignited an internal fire that only one thing could quench. Impatient little hands grabbed his cock and rubbed until he allowed her to guide him to her slick opening. He plunged in without waiting, groaning as her soft heat enveloped him, encasing him in sweet oblivion.

"Oh God, Laci," he moaned, losing his ability to remain in control. "God, you're so tight and wet." So perfect.

"You smell like me," she whispered in his ear, adding with a sultry giggle, "That turns me on."

"Total confession—everything about you turns me on," he admitted in a strained voice as he tried to slow his thrusts. He wanted her to come first or he'd never forgive himself. Grabbing her legs, he hoisted them over his shoulders and rammed himself hard against her G-spot, knowing that it would drive her crazy. He wasn't wrong. Laci cried out, her eyes squeezing shut as her breasts bounced with each thrust. "You like that, baby?" he asked, grunting as he pounded her hard, nearly dying from the pleasure of being inside her. "God, Laci," he choked out as the sensation of pure carnal heaven cut off his vocal cords. "I'm gonna come, girl!"

He lost all reason and within seconds he'd lost his load, too. Spilling inside her hot sheath, his hips pumped as if a demon was working the machinery and he was helpless to control it. His seed burst from his cock in hot jets, and he'd never felt his heart so close to exploding than in that moment. "Oh God, girl," he muttered, barely able to form the words as he collapsed on top of her, pressing soft, weak kisses along her collarbone as they both breathed heavily. The scent of hay and sex filling the air and creating one helluva mental trigger so that every time he walked into this barn, he'd never think of anything aside from Laci—even more so than when he'd been a kid.

And then his brain kicked back in and he asked, "Um, are you… Hell, I should've asked first… I'm sorry, Laci…"

She surprised him with a husky laugh and wrapped her arms around him, saying, "I'm protected. No babies for this girl while she's on tour." He should've been relieved, but for some reason the knowledge fell flat. A baby with Laci. He'd never considered it with anyone else, but…maybe with Laci… No, what the hell was wrong with him? He rolled off her and started to find his clothes, immediately shaken by the completely screwed-up notion that'd somehow wedged itself in his mind. Laci, noting his sudden change in demeanor, frowned as she grabbed her bra. "You okay?"

He forced a grin. "Right as rain, baby," he told her, not wanting to ruin the moment when he didn't even know where the errant thought had come from. He helped her up and then after they'd dressed, they began to walk back to the house. When Laci slipped her hand into his, he closed his fingers over hers, but he didn't know what they were doing aside from confusing the hell out of each other.

Laci flashed him a bright smile as she pulled forward and said before disappearing into the house, "You're not getting out of washing up, Dalton. I'll get dinner, and you clean."

He tipped an imaginary hat her direction, but his smile faded the minute she was behind the front door.

What a fine mess.

It's just sex, a voice argued, but he knew that was a bunch of horseshit.

It'd never been just sex with Laci and it never would be.

And that was what he had to deal with.

Somehow.

12

LACI HUMMED UNDER her breath, that fragment of song coming to her as she served up the pot roast, content for the first time in a long time. Maybe it was the little things that she missed the most and hadn't realized were very important to a country girl like herself. She smiled as Kane exited the bathroom, all cleaned up and looking yummy as ever. What was it about that man that drove her crazy? It was as if there were a trigger inside her that released a whole circus of crazy inside her heart and then it was all about trying to wrangle the monkeys that were tearing stuff up. Except she liked the monkeys and she didn't care what kind of damage she'd end up having to clean up later. Yeah, that was the pure crazy part and she knew it.

Pot roast, red potatoes and green beans, that's good eating right there, she thought with pride as she served up their plates. One thing Cora had taught her was how to plate a good dinner that'll stick to the ribs because hardworking country men needed something real on their forks. "None of that fancy foo-foo stuff," Cora had scoffed.

"The way to a man's heart is through his stomach, you mark my words, Chickpea," Cora had told her one hot summer day while in the kitchen. Laci had grinned, loving the nickname Cora had given her from the minute they'd met. "A man—a real man, mind you—wants meat and potatoes, stuff that goes down to the gut and stays there a while. Some ladies think the way to bend a man is with their pretty face and a lot of this—" Cora wiggled her hips and Laci had laughed "—but they'd be wrong. Good food keeps a man where he belongs."

"So you're saying that if I learn to cook real good, I'll never be alone?" Laci asked.

Cora smiled and smoothed a worn hand over Laci's head with a warm smile and squeezed her chin lightly. "My little Chickpea, I would never steer you wrong. A woman has many talents, many gifts, but her true talent is revealed in the kitchen. Now, grab that sack of flour and bring it over. I'm gonna show you how to properly bread a chicken leg. Ain't nothing better than fried chicken on a summer night and that's the truth, but the secret is in the scald, my sweet girl. All in the scald."

Laci roused herself from the memory and realized Kane was watching her intently. "You okay? You looked like you'd disappeared from the table."

"I did for a minute," Laci admitted, shaking off the reverie before returning to Kane with a smile. "I was just thinking about Cora. Remember how she used to call me Chickpea? I don't know why, but whenever she called me that, I always felt loved. Weird, huh?"

Kane graced her with a smile filled with love for Cora and said, "Nothing weird about that. Cora is a special woman. She has a way of reaching into your heart and finding all the weak spots so she can shore it up with her unique brand of duct tape."

Laci laughed. "You're right. God, I hope she's okay. Have you heard from Warren at all?"

"No, not yet. I thought to give them a call tonight, but I didn't want to pester them in case Cora is resting. I don't know what the treatments are like and all that, so I figured it was best to wait, but I'm getting antsy, too."

Laci nodded, concerned. "She has to pull through. I feel like such a shit for not staying in better contact with them. They're like my family—my only family since Daddy died—but my schedule has been so…well, hectic, you know?"

"Same. I mean, I suspect being on tour's no picnic, though. I'm sure the Bradfords don't hold a grudge against you."

She didn't worry about that. Cora and Warren were loyal to the core. Once they let you in, it would take a nuclear blast to knock you free. But still, she knew where the fault lay and it was with her. There was no excuse for abandoning them the way she had. "I wish I could cut the tour short. I'm done with being in a different hotel every night, a different city by the following night. It's wearing on my nerves something fierce." She rubbed at her temples as a tension headache sprang from nowhere at the mere mention of returning to the tour.

"So cut it short. It's your tour, right?" Kane said, as if that was the answer. Bless his heart, he didn't know the first thing about tour responsibilities, but she didn't hold it against him. When she simply graced him with a patient smile, he frowned and said, "Now, I know you think I'm talking out of my ass but damn it, Laci, you're the star. That ought to come with some kind of privilege, right? You collapsed on the stage in Memphis. What's gonna happen when it happens again? You're playing with fire, girl."

"I wish I could just quit the tour, but there are people relying on me for their livelihood, Kane. I help feed their families. I can't just quit because I'm *tired*," she told him.

He hit her with a stern look. "Exhaustion and fatigue ain't the same and you know it. Your manager isn't doing you any favors by booking you into the ground," he maintained. "Listen, I understand you feel responsible for these people—I get it, I have a payroll, too—but in your case, they know a tour isn't supposed to last forever. If you have to cut your tour short, they'll just find someone else to work for on another tour. And no one is saying you can't ever tour again, just give yourself some breathing room, for crying out loud."

"I wish it were that easy," she said, shaking her head. Why were they arguing? Criminy. She just wanted to put an end to this conversation and go back to enjoying their dinner. "I know what, why don't we go down to the fishing pond and see if we can catch some fireflies. I remember doing that as a kid and there's just something about it that I miss."

Kane shook his head, returning to his plate, and she knew he was swallowing whatever else he had to say on the matter. "Sure, that's fine," he said, around a fork-ful of roast. As he chewed, he closed his eyes, clearly enjoying the food, even if he was bothered by the conversation, and Laci thought to herself, Cora, that crafty old bird, was right. *When all else fails...stuff a man with good food.*

KANE DIDN'T HAVE any right butting his nose into Laci's business, but once the barn door was open, it was real hard to chase after the horses. The idea of Laci going back on tour when she was plainly exhausted rubbed him all sorts of wrong, but what could he do? In the overall picture, he was no one in Laci's world. The truth pinched but he wasn't in a habit of sugarcoating bullshit just because he didn't like the smell. So that left him with one option: swallowing his opinion and letting her run her own life.

And he hated that option.

Laci grabbed her plate and his after he'd finished his last bite and then after they'd washed and put away the dishes, they grabbed some Mason jars and headed outside. Laci slipped her hand into his and they walked into the humid summer night, the sound of cicadas buzzing all around them, and Kane felt his tension draining away. He'd forgotten how soothing that sound was. He lived in the city now, where, although his house wasn't exactly planted in the middle of downtown, the night sounds were nothing the way they were in the country, where nature flanked you on all sides.

"Admit it, this was a good idea," Laci teased, bumping him with her shoulder playfully, and he nodded with a small smile, which she matched with an even bigger one. "I've missed this so much," she said with a sigh as they walked toward the creek that cut its way through the property and fed the pond. As they approached, bullfrogs belched their night song from the reeds and there was something so perfect about the moment that Kane was momentarily pulled back in time to when he and Laci used to come to this very spot for a few hurried kisses and wild, fumbling embraces stolen between chaperoned moments. Laci must've remembered, too, because she cuddled up close to him with a contented sigh that tickled his soul in a way that could only be called dangerous. "I've missed you, Kane. Why'd we lose touch with each other? I've needed you in my life."

They settled on the bank and Kane pulled his boots off, wiggling his toes in the soft, cool grass, taking a moment before answering her. "Life took us in different directions," he said, prepared to leave it at that, but Laci wasn't satisfied with his answer.

"It didn't have to. Why'd you leave me? I know you still care about me, which means you cared about me then, but you still left me behind as if I didn't matter. Why'd you do that, Kane?"

"I thought we were going to catch fireflies," he said, half joking.

"I know. But I've got questions that never got answers and you're here now and I figure it's a good time to get those answers."

He sighed, wishing she'd just leave things be. She wasn't going to like his answer and it was going to ruin their entire evening. A firefly drifted by and he pointed, hoping to distract her. "There you go, your firefly. Better catch it, darlin', before it goes home."

Laci snagged his chin gently and dragged his gaze back to her, serious as a heart attack, and he knew there was no running from the conversation she was meaning to have. That was the thing about Laci, she was damn stubborn when she put her mind to something. He exhaled and gave up any hope of the evening ending well. "Laci, why'd your daddy leave you here every summer so he could go logging?"

She drew back with a frown. "To make money for the winter," she answered. "But you know that."

"Yeah, I do. Your daddy was always looking out for your best interests. Unlike mine who didn't give two shits about me or Rian, your daddy cared."

"Yeah? I know he did. He had his faults but he was a good man," Laci agreed slowly, her confusion obvious. "Where you going with that?"

He exhaled with a rueful chuckle. "I'm not sure you want to know, but since you're doing the asking, I'll answer."

"Okay, then. Out with it," Laci said.

"The truth of the matter is, when your daddy came to me and said that I needed to make myself scarce so you could do what you were meant to do, I knew he was right. You wouldn't have made your dreams come true if I was hanging around like a stone around your neck. I made the choice and I stand by it. Besides, it wasn't completely noble on my part," he admitted. "Part of what I said to you that night was true even though it hurt to say it. I realized that you were going places, going places I couldn't go, and I knew I didn't have what it took to be your backstage man. I don't like to share, Laci. And sharing you with the world? Hell, that's just beyond my understanding or capacity to do."

"My daddy told you to leave me?" she asked, her voice troubled. "But why? Why would he do that? He knew I had feelings for you."

"That's right, and he knew there was no room in your life for those feelings because feelings like that cloud judgment. I don't blame him none for his look-ing out for you—hell, in fact, I respected the man for it, because sometimes the truth is what we need even if it's not dressed the way we want."

"My heart was broken," Laci said, the reproach in her eyes almost unbearable. "How could either of you do that to me?"

"Before you get all twisted up about that, he was right. Look around. You've done real good for yourself and I stand by the choice I made all those years ago."

"I can't believe it," Laci said, clearly hurt. "My own daddy? But why? I don't understand. He always liked you."

He chuckled. "Honey, no man likes the man who's screwing his daughter, no matter how he might say otherwise. But that's okay, I didn't take it personal. Besides, we both loved you and wanted what was best for you."

Her expression changed into one of indignation. "Yeah, that's the point—a choice *you* made. You didn't give me a chance to weigh in on my own future. God-damn it, Kane, other people have been running my life for so long I can't remember what it feels like to make my own damn decisions. I don't even get to decide if I want toast with my eggs anymore. The decision is made for me. No toast. Too many carbs. And I like toast! No, in fact, I *love* toast. Doesn't seem right to have eggs without toast."

"So eat some toast, girl," Kane said, unsure of where this was going. Was she mad about her breakfast or what? "Listen, I can't control who you let run your life. All I can say is that I made a choice for myself, not just you, and I believe, even if you don't, that it was the right one, given the circumstances. Girl, you're top of the charts, killing it out there with legions of fans. You're living the dream. Why would I ever stand in the way of that?"

Laci, frustrated, shook her head. "Don't you get it? I didn't ask you to be noble on my part. I just asked you to love me. Why was that so hard? You walked away before giving me the chance to be a part of that decision. You broke my heart, Kane Dalton, and it took a long time before I got over you."

He wanted to tell her that he'd never gotten over her, but what would that solve? Likely, the admission would only make things worse. "I did what was best," he maintained stubbornly, and she made a small sound of irritation that shouldn't have sounded cute but it did. "C'mere, hothead," he said, pulling her into his arms. Even though she went, everything about her was stiff and rigid. Boy, she was mad, all right. Good thing there weren't any sharp objects lying around. He pressed a kiss to her neck, in the spot he knew drove her crazy, murmuring against her skin, "What's in the past should stay there, baby girl. We have right now. Let's enjoy it while we can."

Laci surprised him when she pulled away and then pushed him to his back to straddle him, still angry and looking hotter than ever. "You're a piece of work. You break my heart, abandon me without once looking back to see if I was all right and then you say, *What's in the past should stay there.* Well, you're wrong, Kane. You're just wrong. I needed you by my side, not running off to play soldier."

He lifted up on his elbows. "I *served* my country. I didn't run off to *play*," he corrected her with a narrowed gaze. "I'm sorry you're unable to think past your own hurt to realize that it was a blessing. We're not meant to be together, honey. That's the plain truth of it. It's not my fault I saw that truth before you did."

She growled and then gripped a handful of his shirt to pull him straight to her mouth. She sealed her lips to his, demanding his full attention as she deepened the kiss, sweeping his mouth with her sassy tongue, and just about the moment when he was ready to shuck their clothes and pound himself into that sweet body, she released him and said, "You lied, Kane. We are meant to be together and it's just your plain bullheaded nonsense that tells you otherwise. You can sleep in the pump house tonight and think about it." Then she climbed off him and walked back to the house, leaving him in the dark with nothing but the fireflies and an empty Mason jar.

Well, hell.

So much for doing the right thing.

13

LACI LEFT KANE in a huff, caught between pissed off and hurt that everyone in her life, since before she even realized, was managing her life as if she were some helpless kitten who couldn't handle a conflict on her own. *Why, Daddy?* The fact that her father had had a hand in pushing Kane away hurt more than a little, but what hurt worse was that Kane had been all too happy to just walk away, using her daddy's objections to their relationship as the reason. She wasn't a stranger to the fact that her daddy didn't want her dating anyone seriously—hell, he'd come out and admitted it to her while they were driving to one of her earliest recordings.

"You need to focus on what's important, girl," her daddy had admonished when she'd been wiping her eyes, crying over leaving the Bradford ranch and leaving Kane the summer she turned seventeen. "That boy, he ain't nothing but a chapter in your life. You're meant to do big things, not hang laundry and bake pies, honey."

"Who's to say I can't do all those things and sing,

too?" she'd retorted, still wrung out from saying good-bye to the boy who'd stolen her heart. "I mean, Kane loves my singing. He'd never stand in my way."

"Trust me, honey, boys like Kane, they grow up to be men that can't be caged. He's never gonna be happy following you around while you shine. He's a good kid, don't get me wrong, and I like that he's always seemed to treat you right, but honey, you're too young to know what your heart really wants. Stick to what is plain in front of your face—your singing talent. Ain't nobody that can sing like you, honey. No one. And Kane, if he loves you, will step aside and let you be who you're meant to be."

"Kane will never leave me," she assured her daddy. "That's a fact. He'd follow me anywhere."

"That's all you need, some guy hanging around distracting you," her daddy grumbled. "No boy is worth your future. Trust me when I say that boys will lead you nowhere. They're all looking for one thing and that has nothing to do with anything but their own selfish needs."

"Daddy," she'd admonished, knowing that Kane was the sweetest, most considerate boy she'd ever known. If anything, he always sacrificed for the people around him. "You don't know Kane like I do."

"I don't have to," he said, glowering. "I know all about boys and even more about men. The thing is, honey, you believe the best in people and that's one of your sweetest qualities, but I'm not hamstrung by the same quality. Your future is destined to be more than making babies and sweet-potato pie for your man. Your star is so much brighter and I aim to make sure that nothing stands in your way."

"Kane's not standing in my way," she insisted. "If anything, he's the one pushing me, just like you. He wants me to be a famous singer."

"Well, then, he can enjoy seeing you on television and go on his merry way."

"I love him, Daddy," Laci said, annoyed and hurt that her daddy was being so disagreeable. "I truly do and nothing's gonna change that."

He graced her with a short derisive look that she found insulting as he said, "You don't know what love is, sweetheart. Not true love. You're too young, and besides, there's more to life than love."

"How can you say that when you loved Mama the way you did?"

At the mention of his beloved wife, he scowled. "Not the same and don't go using my past against me."

"You and Mama were just as young as me and Kane and I know you loved each other."

"Yeah, and that love didn't get us nowhere but heartache and misery," he said. "Sometimes I think it was a blessing your mama died when she did. Do you think she'd like to live the way we do? Living off the scraps of others? Being gypsies from one season to another? I can't do nothing about our finances, but you can. You got the talent to pull us out of this mud pit and that's what you're gonna do. No more distractions, girl. No more talk of boys and love. I won't listen and I won't let you throw away your life for something so fleeting."

"I can't believe what a pigheaded mule you're being,"

Laci said, her tears starting fresh. Her daddy was her biggest champion, her hero most days, but today he was so damn mean-hearted that she almost didn't know him. "Well, you can think what you want, but Kane will never leave my side. We love each other and nothing's gonna change that."

"Girl, trust in your daddy. I would never steer you wrong. Now, stop your crying over that boy and warm up your voice. We got one shot with this big-time producer and we don't want to disappoint him."

"Fine," she'd said with a glower. Laci hadn't wanted to sing but somehow she'd found the ability to focus. By the time they'd reached their destination, Laci could hit every high note and belt out every chord. Suffice to say, she'd aced that audition and had made her first real recording connection. Riding high on her success, she couldn't wait to tell Kane, only to find out through the Bradfords that Kane had left the same day to join the military. Her mouth had dropped open and her heart had contracted as the words had registered. Kane had left her. Kane—the boy who'd sworn to go wherever she went—had abandoned her. Just like that.

That was the day she'd learned the heartbreaking lesson that love wasn't enough.

At least it hadn't been for Kane.

KANE HAD EVERY intention of sleeping in the pump house, but his feet had other plans, and before he knew it, he was heading to Laci's bedroom all fired up and ready to say his piece.

He pushed open the door and went straight to Laci,

ignoring her fierce stare and unwelcome vibe. He didn't care if she didn't want him there. She was going to listen and that was that. "I was a kid faced with a choice that I never imagined happening to someone like me," he said. "I didn't like it but the facts were clear, you were going places and if I hung around, all I'd be was a distraction and I couldn't have that on my conscience. I left because it was the only way I could make myself do the right thing, but don't think for a minute that leaving didn't leave its scars because it did."

"No one could ever have convinced me to leave you," Laci said, hurt and angry. "But you caved at the first sign of trouble."

"That's not how I see it. I made the right choice for both of us."

"Well, that's not how I see it."

"Fair enough. I guess we'll have to agree to disagree then and move on."

Outrage colored her voice as she exclaimed, "Move on? To what? You're not going to just sweep this under the rug and let it be because you don't want to talk about it. We're going to have the conversation we should've had years ago and we're going to have it right now!"

"Like hell we are," he countered, pulling her into his arms. "Nothing can be done about the past, babe. Best to leave it there. All that matters is the now." And then as she opened her mouth to likely skewer him, he silenced her the only way he knew how. She stiffened against his carnal onslaught, but soon enough she softened in his arms and they were tumbling to the bed. There was something about Laci that made him insatiable, sparking an itch that was always just out of reach, which made him need more, and as she twisted in his arms, kissing, squeezing, clinging to him even as he ravaged her body with his touch, he knew a lifetime would never be enough with this woman.

Pulling Laci to her knees, he sank into that sweet, slippery heat, losing himself between the dewy folds that promised heaven with each hard thrust. He wanted to sink so deep that they no longer recognized where each started and ended because they were one. The sound of their harsh breathing, guttural moans and slapping flesh filled the air as did the musk from their love-making, and Kane knew only Laci in that moment. Talk about living in the now. He would gladly live in this moment for the rest of his life if he were able. No uncomfortable reality to contend with, just the complete bliss found between the hot legs of the sexiest woman he'd ever known.

Laci moaned, her body shaking with each thrust as he found her G-spot and hammered it hard. He knew just the way Laci liked to be taken and he thrilled at the privilege of that knowledge. Within moments, Laci gasped, clutching at the comforter, crying out his name as she came and he quickly followed with a brutal explosion of his own. He collapsed beside her, his legs hanging off the bed as his heart threatened to shatter. His spent cock still pulsed from the epic orgasm and it was a long moment before he could speak.

But it was Laci who spoke first, her voice hoarse and throaty as she said, "That's an unfair way to end an argument."

He climbed fully on the bed and gathered her in his arms, ready for sleep. "All's fair in love and war, sweetheart."

She nestled against him and murmured, "That was a battle, not the war."

And he knew for certain, this conversation was far from over. But at least, for the moment, she wasn't sending him back to the pump house.

That was something, right?

14

THE FOLLOWING MORNING Kane and Laci rose early, and while Kane was out tending to the cattle and horses, Laci spent time in the kitchen, happy to be simply domestic. The phone rang and she picked it up without hesitation. When she heard Warren's voice on the other end, she shocked him with an exuberant hello.

"Warren! It's me, Laci," she said, smiling at Warren's momentary confusion. "Bet you didn't expect to hear from me on the other line, huh?"

"Laci? What you doing, girl? Aren't you supposed to be on tour or something?"

"Taking a brief break to get my head on straight. The road's a terrible place to stay for too long," she answered, cradling the phone against her shoulder while she molded piecrust with her hands. "Kane told me all about Cora… How's our girl doing? And why didn't you tell me about her being sick? Jiminy, Warren, I would've flown in the best doctors in the world to tend to Cora if you'd just asked."

"I know you would, little lady, and you're a sweet one for even suggesting it, but I take care of my own, you know that."

"That's silly, you old goat. Cora's like a grandma to me and I can't stand the idea of her suffering none when it can be prevented with a single phone call. I've got the resources and nothing to spend it on. Let me help you out a bit."

"Listen, I appreciate the gesture, but we're doing just fine. Keep your money and invest it. The last thing you need is to start throwing away cash like there's no tomorrow and end up broke like those professional sports stars who don't know their asses from a hole in the ground when it comes to spending their money. Spending it on fast cars and loose women…that's a quick ticket to poverty."

She rolled her eyes. "I promise you I'm not out spending money on fast cars and loose women and I would consider it my honor and privilege to help cover Cora's treatment costs."

"I said no, girl. Leave it be," Warren said sharply, shocking Laci with his curt tone. Warren had never spoken to her that way. She blinked back sudden tears and was momentarily speechless, which was a first because she rarely ran out of words on any particular subject that she could remember. "I don't mean to hurt your feelings, but I've said my piece on the subject and that's final. It's real good to hear from you, Laci. Feel free to make yourself at home and don't give Kane too much grief. He's a good man," he said, pausing a beat to say, "Speaking of…is Kane around?"

She found her voice to answer. "He's in the barn. I'll get him for you."

"No, no, I don't want to bother him when he's working. Just have him call. Here's a number he can reach me at. I had to get one of those dang-gummed cell phones because Cora's treatment takes hours and they have to be able to reach me at a moment's notice. God-damn gadgets…that's no way for a man to live his life. I miss my land and my animals. Everything okay at the ranch?"

Laci wiped at her tears and nodded, even though Warren couldn't see her nod her head. She spoke up, saying, "Yeah, real good. Kane and I are catching up on lost time. I can't believe Jasper's still around and wouldn't you know it, he still remembers Kane? It's the darnedest thing I ever seen."

"Horses are smart," Warren said unnecessarily, which made Laci feel they were just stretching out the conversation in the hopes of smoothing out the jagged edge of the earlier conversation, but no matter how many benign topics they touched on, nothing would erase the hurt in her heart at her help being rebuffed so sharply. Her gaze drifted to the new appliances and she wondered if she'd made a huge error in judgment in buying them without their approval. She bit her lip, worried. Maybe she ought to mention it? No, she knew Warren's reaction would be negative at this point because that's where he seemed to live at the moment, so she kept that information to herself.

"Cora will be real happy to know you're at the house,"

Warren said. "I just wish you'd dropped by sooner, maybe caught us before we left."

"I know," she acknowledged with a guilty murmur. "But this was really unexpected. I sort of…collapsed and then ran away from my manager. It's just a temporary thing but I needed some time to myself to think things out."

"Everything okay between you and Kane?" Warren asked. "Last time I checked, you weren't even friends anymore."

Laci thought of how to answer that question honestly. What were she and Kane doing? Were they friends? Were they more than that? She hated the term *friends with benefits* and she was pretty sure Kane would hate it, too, but she didn't know that what was happening between them was easily defined. "We're catching up on lost time," she finally answered, going with a variation of the truth. "But we share a common concern and that's for Cora. Please keep us updated, okay?"

"Of course, sweetheart. And I'm sorry for being so gruff with you earlier. It's just hard. Cora's a tough old bird, but this treatment…it's taking its toll. Can't hardly watch to see what it's doing to her. I think I might've made a mistake in bringing her here."

Fresh tears pricked her eyes at his admission. "It's okay. I understand. And I'm sure the treatment is doing Cora some good. Those doctors know what they're doing. You just got to keep the faith."

"I'm trying. I really am."

The lump returned to her throat, but she tried to reassure Warren in the only way she knew how. "Don't you worry about the ranch. Kane will keep it running smooth for you, and if there's anything you can think of that I can do for you, please don't hesitate to ask."

"Thanks, I'll keep that in mind," Warren said, even though Laci knew with a certain amount of frustration that he wouldn't ask. Warren was old-school. It was something she loved about him, but it came with its drawbacks, too. He suddenly perked up to add, "Hey, since you're in town, you ought to check out the harvest festival. Should start tonight. I remember your loving that little carnival."

The Woodsville Harvest Festival was the little town's big shindig, where home-baked goodies, crafts, carnival rides and nostalgia were everywhere. She'd even won a blue ribbon or two with Cora's help with a few of her pies—peach and blueberry, to be exact—and, of course, she and Kane had sneaked quite a few kisses on the Ferris wheel.

"I'll see if Kane wants to go," she said, wondering what Kane's reaction would be. He'd never been a huge fan, only going when they were kids because she'd begged and pleaded. Kane had more bad memories of Woodsville than anyone she knew and he didn't find the same appeal in the country carnival, but maybe he'd do it for her. She said her goodbyes to Warren and then, after popping her cherry pie into the oven, she went to find Kane.

She found him securing the gate for the cattle as they ambled in for their morning meal. A few clouds scuttled across the hazy sky and a cool breeze swept a few turning leaves from the trees, heralding the coming season. Laci drank in the beauty and perfection of the moment with a heavy heart. Soon enough, she'd find herself back on a tour bus, eating up the miles between cities, and her life would become a blur.

She couldn't imagine Kane cooped up in a bus for hours on end, only to stand in the shadows while she performed. She supposed her daddy had been right; a man like Kane wasn't meant to be caged. And she'd never want him to be. That's what she liked most about the man—his strength and virile presence.

He caught her standing there and waved before coming toward her. Muscle rippled beneath his worn T-shirt as it clung to his perfect form and Laci caught her breath. He was, without a doubt, the sexiest man she'd ever laid eyes on. Funny how, even though years had passed since they were kids, learning about physical attraction and all that came with it, that little tingle in her belly whenever she saw him had never gone away. It was still there—reminding her that Kane, for all the improbability of things working out, would only ever be the man for her.

KANE SAW—NO, that wasn't accurate, he felt—Laci standing there, watching him, and a grin found him easily. The cattle were happily chowing down on their feed and the horses were taken care of, as well. Dundee, Warren's old yellow Lab, loped alongside Kane, happy to be out in the field, sniffing and exploring, though he was half-blind and probably half-deaf, too, but still happy. "C'mon, old man," he said to Dundee, rolling his eyes when the goofy dog stared up at him with his tongue lolling out and what looked like a grin on his mug. "Warren must have a knack for keeping animals going long past their expiration date. You're a damn miracle dog to still be alive after all this time."

Dundee's response to that was an enthusiastic bark, but as far as Kane knew, the dog couldn't tell what or who he was barking at because then he shambled off, going a little sidewise, back to the house where he knew a nice comfy bed awaited him—and probably a treat.

He met Laci on the porch and she gave him a fresh sweet tea to wet his whistle. He could count on his hand the things he missed about living in the South and sweet tea was one of them. He finished his tea in a few gulps and leaned in for a quick kiss. "That hit the spot. The humidity is kicking my ass. I'm used to a dry heat now, not this wet, collapse-your-lungs-when-you-breathe stuff."

She laughed. "It brings back memories. Honestly, my home base is Los Angeles, so I know what you're saying."

He cast a surprised glance at Laci. "You live in LA?"

"Well, as much as you can call it living. I feel as if I'm hardly there enough to qualify as actually living there." He took a moment to process that. He'd been living in Los Angeles for years and he'd never realized that Laci was in the same city. Now, granted, he also made a point to avoid any reference to Laci and he wasn't one to peruse the gossip rags, so missing that piece of information wasn't too surprising, but still... it rocked him a little that they'd always been relatively close to one another.

Laci frowned at his sudden silence. "You okay?"

"Just surprised, is all. I didn't realize you lived in the same city."

She risked a shy glance before admitting, "When you mentioned that you and Rian were working in SoCal, I wanted to ask if you lived there, too, but it didn't seem appropriate to ask, you know? I mean, there's so many questions between us, I hardly know which ones are safe to ask and which ones I ought to leave be."

"You can ask me anything," he told her quietly, and he meant it. He wouldn't shy away from her questions even if the answer wouldn't do him any favors. "You were right earlier…some of these questions should've been answered a long time ago."

"Thank you, that means a lot," she said, her gaze softening. "You know, I've dreamed up all sorts of scenarios between us, but none were as perfect as the real deal right now."

He smiled, but her admission cut. If things were perfect, they wouldn't be ignoring the fact that reality was waiting to bust up their happy peace like a bully in the school yard, punching his palm with a gleeful expression. "I'm all yours, sugar," he told her with a playful grin to cover the pain in his heart. "I'm at your mercy."

Her delighted smile warmed and soothed as she said playfully, "Is that so? Well then, I might as well ask every question I've ever wondered, seeing as I have a captive audience."

"Be gentle," he begged, and she laughed. He sobered and said, "Okay, what do you want to know?"

"How'd you end up in California, of all places? I

would've thought maybe Montana or someplace with mountains and plenty of space. I know how you value your privacy. Los Angeles isn't what you'd call a mecca for guarding your privacy. I should know…I've had three people arrested for trying to climb my gate."

"You really need better security," he said, frowning. "What kind of alarm system are you using? If it's the Iron King 2000, it's crap. It's the easiest to disarm and a virtual joke, but every celebrity client I have seems to buy into their propaganda. Personally, I always suggest—"

She silenced him with a finger against his lips. "I don't want to talk about alarm systems," she said, shaking her head. "I want to talk about how you ended up in the same city as me and I never knew it."

He settled down, realizing he'd been way too eager to jump into a whole different conversation than what they were inching toward, but Laci wanted answers and he'd promised he would give them. "I moved there after I left the military. It seemed the best place for me and Rian to start up our business. It was either LA or New York and neither of us wanted to deal with New York winters, so we settled on SoCal."

"Do you like it?"

He shrugged. "It's all right. I like that everything's within driving distance that I need, but I wish I had more open space. That's one thing I haven't gotten used to…all the people."

"Growing up in the country, you take certain things for granted."

"Like being able to breathe," he quipped, and she

grinned. It felt good to joke even though they were both processing the information they were sharing in their own way. He supposed she was just as startled as he that they'd always been so geographically close to one another. "You know, I always thought you would've picked a place in the South as your home base," he admitted.

"Like you, Los Angeles is just convenient. Can't say I love it, but I have a small ranch in Ojai that's far enough away from the city with enough acreage for some semblance of privacy. It's the best that I can get under the circumstances, but it's nowhere near as homey as this place right here."

His place was small and functional with a parcel that was just big enough to justify the millions he'd paid for it, but, just like Laci said, it was nowhere near what he'd really like.

She went to him and looped her arms around him. "Maybe you could come visit me sometime," she suggested, brushing a kiss across his lips. "Would you like that?"

He sighed, knowing there was no good answer to that question. If all things were equal, he wouldn't hesitate to pick up where they left off here in Kentucky, but then what? Heartache and misery. He'd hate the idea of her going off on tour, leaving him for months on end, and he wasn't about to hop a tour bus to be her backstage boyfriend. "Let's just keep it simple for now," he said gruffly, and she nodded, trying to hide the disappointment in her eyes.

"Of course," she said, forcing a smile as she briskly

switched gears. "In that case, tonight we're going to the Woodsville Harvest Festival."

"What?" he groaned, unable to believe what'd popped from her mouth. "Are you serious?"

"As a heart attack. I used to love the harvest festival and I thought you did, too."

"Yeah, when we were kids and we could sneak away for a few stolen kisses." He tightened his grip on her with a seductive smile. "But we're not kids anymore and I don't have to steal what I've got in my arms right now. Let's just see what kind of trouble we can get into right here."

"But I can't get homemade candied apples right here," she countered, laughing when he nuzzled her neck. "C'mon, it'll be fun. I'll even let you steal a kiss on the Ferris wheel for old time's sake."

She was really serious about this? He pulled away with a subtle frown. "You're not kidding?"

"Nope. Besides, we need a change of scenery. We've been cooped up here on the ranch for days. Time to get some fresh air, so to speak. Can you be ready by six?"

He could tell by the firm set of her jaw that she had her mind set. When he thought of the town of Woodsville, he had nothing good to fall back on, except for the harvest festival, but only because he'd been a lovestruck kid with hearts in his eyes, and if Laci had asked him to rope the moon, he would've tried. But other than that…a small-town festival, filled with the small-town cronies who'd done nothing to lift a finger to help him or his brother? Nope, not big on that idea. However, he knew just as he was standing there that he'd go because Laci wanted it.

Some things hadn't changed—he just couldn't say no to the woman.

15

LIKE ANTS SPILLING out of a colony, everyone and their grandmother came to sell their wares, socialize and have a good time at the Woodsville Harvest Festival.

Kane and Laci stepped out of the truck, and Kane prepared himself for a mildly unpleasant walk down memory lane until Laci caught his attention with a blinding smile and he momentarily forgot why he hadn't wanted to come.

Maybe if she wasn't so damn hot. The woman had cornered the market on sexy, and if there ever was a stereotypical country-girl look, Laci had nailed it. Cowboy boots, short white skirt and a cute blouse with her hair tied up in a bandanna, Laci looked like something out of one of her own music videos.

Kane paid for their tickets and, as they walked through the arched entryway and into the festival, he was immediately assaulted by memories. To a passing stranger, Woodsville was a place where the South lived and breathed in all its colorful splendor, pretty as a picture and just about as chock-full of Americana as one could get without landing on a movie set where everything was carefully placed and planned for effect. But Woodsville was the real deal. People didn't lock their doors at night and it wasn't unheard of to hear tell that a barn raising was happening, but it wasn't all maple syrup and corn-husk dolls; there was an ugly side that he was well acquainted with. The poverty level was abysmal and those living under that federally recognized line of misery were often overlooked and forgotten because they were country folk who kept to themselves, which also meant that if there was abuse happening, of any sort, it would just keep on happening because there wasn't anyone who was going to step in to stop it. And guess where Kane and his brother had landed on that line? On the messed-up side.

Laci, sensing the tension, curled her arm around his biceps and pressed herself closer to him. Just having her on his arm had a calming effect, but he wasn't only on edge for himself—he was worried about someone recognizing Laci and causing a scene. He was no one but she was a bona fide country star. Sooner or later, if they kept pressing their luck, someone was going to recognize her. And then what? He didn't like the idea of people clamoring around Laci as if it were their right to do so. Given his line of work, it should've come easier to him, but he didn't care about his clients the way he cared about Laci. When he was working, it was all about the job. He wasn't emotionally involved in the clients' lives. And he sure as hell wasn't sleeping with them.

"You're rigid as an oak plank," she teased. "What

are you so afraid of? You're a successful man with your own business and there's no one here who can take that away from you. Just try to enjoy yourself."

Laci knew of his demons, his nightmares, and the fact that she was readily on his side, defending him, warmed his heart, but he had to come clean. "It's not me I'm worried about. What if someone recognizes you?" he asked, voicing his fear. "What am I supposed to do? What if someone gets crazy?"

"Let's not borrow trouble. Cora used to say, 'Don't build bridges for rivers you don't have to cross yet,'" she said, smiling, not the least bit concerned. "I'm here with you and that's all that matters. Besides, I doubt anyone will recognize me."

He didn't know about that. People would have to be damn blind not to recognize her but he supposed there was nothing he could do until the situation came up, so why ruin the moment? "Okay, I'll follow your lead."

She brightened. "Excellent. Then I say the first order of business is getting a candied apple. You would not believe how much I've craved Woodsville candied apples. I swear, there's something magic in those apples because I've been to countless states and fairs and there's never been a single one to measure up to those delicious goodies they sell here at this festival."

Her enthusiasm softened him up a bit and he realized he'd do almost anything to see her smile. So he'd just have to keep a watchful eye so that Laci could have a good time. "Then a candied apple you shall have. Let's go find one."

They wandered around the festival, stopping here

and there, found the candied-apple booth and then just when he thought Laci might want to call it a night, she dragged him to the Ferris wheel. He groaned, eyeing the contraption without a whole lot of confidence and said, "The Ferris wheel? Look at that thing. It looks like a health hazard. It's probably held together with string and bubble gum."

She laughed and tugged at him. "Don't be such a spoilsport. I'm sure it's fine. It'll be an adventure."

"I don't need adventure," he grumbled, still eyeing the ride with mistrust. "Did I mention I get plenty of an adrenaline rush in my job? I don't really feel the need to tempt fate and board that rolling lawsuit."

"Oh, yes you are and you are going to kiss me at the top just like you did when we were teenagers."

He caught her gaze and couldn't help the smile creeping onto the edges of his mouth. The girl knew just how to push his buttons.

"Do you have a problem with that?" she teased.

"Far be it from me to keep you from what you want. Ferris wheel it is."

"You're adorable when you pretend to be a pushover," she said, giggling.

The night air was filled with laughter, savory country smells, the buzzing activity of countless individual ongoing events, and Kane wondered if he'd been holding on to anger for too long. The festival wasn't half-bad and so far the night had been pretty enjoyable. They climbed into their bucket and began their slow ascent to the top. The stars twinkled in the night sky, as if winking at them both, and Kane was sucked into the sweetness of the moment.

"I believe the lady wanted a kiss," he reminded her softly as he leaned in to press his lips against hers. She grinned and kissed him back. Their tongues danced lightly with one another, teasing, exploring, much like when they were teenagers, and Kane's heart beat as quickly as it had back then. He pulled away, happy to see the haze in her eyes from his kiss and said, "I guess memory lane's not so bad, after all."

"Not at all. So far it's been my favorite place to visit," she murmured. "Tell me why it's taken this long?"

"Do you want the nice answer or the real answer?"

"I'm not sure. It's been such a wonderful night, maybe I'll take the nice answer."

He chuckled. "Probably a good decision. Let's say we both know what we have is special but not meant to last. And maybe we were just saving ourselves the inevitable heartache."

"Or maybe we were both too angry and hurt—or afraid—to ask the questions that needed to be asked of one another."

"It's possible." He didn't want to ruin the night and he knew that if they continued to pick at that wound, something would gush, but he couldn't help wondering if these were the things they should've said years ago. "I never forgot about you. How could I? It's like you were branded on my heart and there was no scraping that sucker off. Not a day went by that I didn't think of you. But eventually I got busy with my own life. I saw other women—nothing lasted—but I blamed the job even though I knew in my heart it was always because you were still in there. It was hard to come to terms with that but I had to."

"I know what you mean. For so long I've been so busy with my career, driving to one specific destination in my mind until I completely lost track of what the destination was in the first place. I feel like I've made it but then I second-guess myself because my manager, Trent, keeps telling me that if I'm not out there, people will forget about me. I've worked too hard to lose it all now."

"And just what exactly would you be losing? Your voice? Your voice is yours forever. You'll be singing tomorrow just as you were singing yesterday. That will never change. But if you're chasing after fame? Yeah, fame fades. That's just the ego, sweetheart. I can't tell you how many clients I've worked with who busted their tails to get to a certain place in their life only to lose it all because they were too busy trying to create a lifestyle that couldn't realistically be maintained. What are you looking for, Laci? You have to know that before you keep chasing your tail."

"Honestly, I don't know what I'm looking for anymore. When it all started I just wanted to sing. But now, everything's all twisted up in what I think I need and what I want. I don't even know anymore."

"That's half your problem right there. If what you're saying is all you ever wanted to do was sing, then do that. Just sing."

"It's not that simple. It may have started out that way but now I have a payroll. I have people who depend on me. I can't just sing like I used to, without a thought about how much the venue is going to offer me. Some-where along the line life got a lot more complicated. I mean, I would love to sing at a place like this. Smaller venues are so much more intimate and you can feel the vibe from the crowd, you can practically smell the sweat from the backs of their necks and it's awesome. I see the smiles on their faces, the joy in their eyes. That's what makes me happy. The bigger venues are… sometimes overwhelming. The lights are blinding and the noise is deafening. My body is vibrating for an hour after I leave the stage and even though I'm wearing a headset, I swear my ears have gone half-deaf from being onstage. I don't mean to complain, but…I don't know, I'm just tired."

"No," he disagreed. "Life has always been compli-cated, but your love of singing wasn't. You've got a gift, Laci. And it ain't going nowhere. Stop driving yourself into the ground for a prize you're not even sure you want to win."

Gotta love that country wisdom. Since when had Kane become so smart? Sexy and wise? Damn, he's the whole package. If only it were as simple as he sug-gested. "I have to finish the tour. If I don't finish, I'll be liable for breach of contract and I could be sued for millions. There's a lot at stake. I wouldn't be able to live with myself if I screwed over the people who work so hard for me."

"There has to be a happy middle. You just need to negotiate with your manager. Celebrity singers cancel tours all the time and sometimes for stupid, inane reasons. In fact, Rian worked for a rap singer who canceled his entire tour because he was bored with road life. Of course, his PR team spun it into a story about the guy suffering from vocal cord strain, but that wasn't the truth. Here's the thing, no one cares about the truth. No one. Particularly in the business you're in. I'm not saying you have to screw everyone over. I'm just saying you need to start standing up for yourself."

She knew he was right. But it was hard to hear. Before her daddy died, he'd been the one to drive her career. And before he'd died, he passed the reins to Trent. Daddy had drilled into her head how lucky they were to land someone like Trent Blackstone to manage her career.

And Daddy had been right, Trent had made her a lot of money. But he was ruthless and sort of an unfeeling bastard at times. Simone hated him, and Audrey sure as hell wasn't sending him a Christmas card anytime soon. So why did she hold on to him? Was it all about the money? What if she had to sell her ranch in Ojai or downsize that huge house in Los Angeles? Would she care?

She thought of the Bradford ranch and how happy and homey it felt and she knew without having to say out loud that she wouldn't miss any of that crap. She could be just as happy in a small house as she could in a palatial mansion. More so, even. She'd only bought that huge house in LA because Trent had assured her that it looked good for entertaining. Yet, she hadn't actually done any entertaining in that house because she was too busy touring! So what was the point of having all this money if she never got to enjoy any of it? Was she supposed to stay on the hamster wheel until she died? Uncertainty kept her from knowing her own mind and she hated the feeling of teetering on a ledge blindfolded.

"Trent is a good man," she said, the words leaving her mouth as if on autopilot because she didn't know how to defend the choices of her life lately. "He's just doing what's best for my career."

"Screw your career. What about you?"

What did he just say? She blinked, offended. "Screw my career? Are you serious? I worked my ass off to get where I am today and you want me to throw it away? What if I said that to you?"

"My career is not trying to kill me," he pointed out. "You dropped from exhaustion at your last concert."

"And you run the risk of being shot at in your career choice," she countered, bristling. "I don't appreciate you tearing down my career choice just because it doesn't jibe with what you wanted for me."

He did a double take. "What are you talking about? I *walked away* from you so that you could build your damn career. I stepped aside so I wouldn't ever be in your way. Don't give me that. However, I never imagined that I was stepping aside so that someone else could step in and run you into the ground."

Why were they fighting yet again? For Pete's sake, was this their curse? To always bicker and pick at each other if they weren't in bed? They hadn't always been so adversarial. At one time, Kane had been her biggest supporter; she had to remember that. She took a moment to dial back her own anger so she could think reasonably again. "Look, I don't want to fight. I just don't like when you say things like that. I've made a lot of sacrifices and I don't like the idea of someone coming in and crapping all over my life's work."

"I didn't crap on your work. I love when you sing," he said, glowering for a long moment until he grudgingly admitted, "I didn't think it was possible to wear out a CD, but I think I did with your first album. I played it so much in private that Rian declared a moratorium on Laci McCall until your new album came out."

Oh, that warmed her heart ridiculously so. Her sinuses tingled and she knew tears weren't far behind. "How'd Rian know you were playing it if it was done in private?" she asked.

"Because we shared an apartment when we were first out of the military and the walls were thin between bedrooms."

She smiled and waited until she knew her voice wouldn't crack and said, "That means a lot to me. I'd always hoped…that maybe you were listening somewhere out there. Track ten…it's about you."

His gaze held hers and until he ducked his head, possibly to hide the blush of pleasure as he said, "I kinda figured. Or at least…I thought, maybe."

She laughed and cuddled up to him. "Okay, secret's out. 'Country Boy' is all you, Kane Dalton."

The Ferris wheel creaked to a stop at the very top and Laci admitted with a deep breath, "I didn't mean to get so fired up. When you say things like *screw your career*, it sparks something crazy inside me and before I know it, I'm saying all sorts of hotheaded things."

He took a moment before answering and she appreciated that he was taking his time because that told her he wanted to say it right. "I would never mock your work. I just don't like the idea of you being taken advantage of by the people who are supposed to be looking out for you. It makes me feel like shit that I'm not the one protecting you, looking out for you. Feels like it should've been my job."

Annnnd, her heart just melted. What a sweet, caring man. The fact that he felt that way about her...well, it did something to her. Something deep and meaningful. But she needed to clarify so he could stop worrying. He didn't deserve that kind of stress on her account. "No one is taking advantage of me," she assured him. "I promise. I will talk to Trent about my tour schedule and get him to dial it back. It's my fault for not speaking up. I'm sure once I talk to Trent he'll understand and want to do what's right for me. He's a good guy. I know I'm not painting him out to be very nice, but he really is, he's just very focused on the end result and sometimes he loses sight of the people that make it happen."

"Well, we'll see about that. I don't know the guy, but I don't like him already. The fact that he wanted to put you back on tour right after you collapsed doesn't make me want to go shake his hand. Frankly, it makes me want to punch him out."

Oh, good Lord. She couldn't have Kane punching out her manager. "Please don't hurt my manager. I can't see how that will make things better."

Kane shrugged. "It might make me feel better. But out of respect for you, I'll keep my hands to myself."

"Thank you." She leaned in closer with a sweet smile. "Can we go back to kissing now?"

He grinned and pulled her close. "Gladly. Talk is overrated anyway."

16

KANE AND LACI had just managed to make a full loop of the festival before someone recognized her. Kane was the first to realize the woman was staring a little too hard at Laci as she was trying to win a stuffed teddy bear. Then a large crowd started to assemble. Kane didn't want to cut short the fun, but he was becoming uncomfortable with the way the woman became animated with her circle of friends, pointing and gasping.

Kane leaned over to whisper in Laci's ear, "I think the jig is up. You've been spotted." And when Laci looked up to see what Kane was talking about, he knew by her expression that things were about to get real. Kane kicked into protective mode, gripping her by the elbow and guiding her quickly away from the building crowd. But within moments, people were pointing and exclaiming as if the queen of England had suddenly shown up and, before they knew it, there were cameras and camera phones being stuck in Laci's face with pleas and demands to get her autograph or a photo with them.

"Back off," he finally had to growl, warding off an overeager person who had thrust a camera into Laci's face. "Show some respect. I'm not shoving a camera in your family's face as you try to enjoy a nice evening at the festival."

"Hey, celebrities are fair game. That's the price they pay for being famous," an obnoxious man spouted off. "Besides, tabloids will pay big money for candid shots of celebrities like her."

"Yeah, well, you're just going to have to find a real job because Laci's not here to fund your lifestyle."

Laci tugged at Kane's shirt, urging him to go. "Come on, let's go. He's just a jerk, and I'm used to it."

"Well, I'm not used to it." He glared at the man. "Back off before I teach you some manners."

"Yeah, tough guy? Go ahead and try."

Laci pleaded with Kane, "Don't do anything. These kinds of people deliberately provoke so they can earn a payout. Settling in court is the way they make their money. Let's just go. I've had enough of the festival anyway."

Kane knew she was right. He'd counseled many clients on that very thing, but usually he was the cool head in these situations. Not this time. His blood was boiling. He hated the idea of random people thinking they had the right to badger Laci simply because she sang songs that people enjoyed. "Go harass someone else."

He grabbed Laci's hand and they walked away quickly, going to the truck and climbing in. His heart was hammering, almost painfully, and his adrenaline was racing. This was exactly what he counseled his clients not to do—don't get emotional. And yet, here he was, gripping the steering wheel, wishing it were the guy's neck. "Why do people have to be such assholes?" he asked, knowing there was no answer. "I can't believe what people will do to another human being for a buck. Makes me sick."

"That was nothing. Sometimes people get downright ugly. They feel entitled to know everything about a celebrity's life. I've even had a few death threats," she admitted with a shaky laugh. He looked at her sharply and she was quick to reassure him, "Trent had them checked out and everything was fine. They were just crazies."

"The crazies are the ones who will follow through with those threats. Trust me, I know something about this. I'm in the protection business. What kind of bodyguards does your manager have placed on the tour?"

She shrugged. "I haven't a clue. I let Trent take care of that stuff."

Kane scowled. "The more I know about this guy the more I think he's an asshole. And incompetent. Death threats should always be taken seriously. That's why they're a felony."

Laci sighed with a yawn. "I can't spend all my time worrying about who might potentially be out there wanting to hurt me. I would go insane. You realize that I sing to sold-out venues and there are millions of people out there who want a piece of me? It's impossible to weed out every potentially dangerous person who might be in the crowd. I understand that's the risk that I take."

"But you can mitigate that risk. You need a competent protection staff."

"I'm sure Trent has excellent bodyguards working for me. It's not like he would purposefully put me in danger."

"Wouldn't he? The funny thing about celebrities… sometimes their value goes up when they're dead. Particularly when they die a tragic death."

"Oh, come on, Kane…you're really not suggesting…?" She couldn't even finish the sentence; it seemed too absurd to her, but Kane wasn't so sure. He didn't know this Trent character, but he did know that Laci had a trusting spirit and if she was in danger, she'd never see it coming in someone she considered part of her inner circle.

She yawned again and said, "Enough of that kind of talk. I'm tired and I don't have the strength to argue with you. Let's just put a pin in it until morning, okay?"

"Whatever you say," he said, agreeing to let the conversation rest, not because he was ready to stop but because he could tell Laci was still fighting extreme fatigue in spite of the rest she'd gotten since arriving at the ranch. Putting her to bed and climbing in beside her sounded better than arguing anyway.

LACI NEEDED TO wind down. Her nerves were stretched taut after what'd happened at the festival. She was so accustomed to the intrusion into her private life that she barely let it register any longer, but experiencing it through Kane's eyes made her realize that her life was spiraling out of control. Impulsively, she went to Kane and pulled him straight to her mouth, sealing hers to his with a hungry, almost desperate kiss. After a long, lingering moment, they broke apart, leaving Kane to gaze at her quizzically.

"Not that I'm complaining, but…what was that for?" He paused a moment before asking, "Are you okay?"

No. She braved a smile for his sake. "I'm great. But you know what I would love?" He waited for her answer and she grinned mischievously as she said, "A bath. I want to soak in that big, claw-foot tub and I want you to join me."

"I don't think the tub is big enough for us both," Kane said with faint concern.

"Sure it is. I'm pretty certain I'll fit perfectly if I lie against you."

He swallowed hard and she bit back a knowing grin. Oh yes, he just popped a boner. "Are you game?"

"You, naked? I'll go anywhere. Hell, I'd squeeze myself into a cardboard box if it meant being shoved up against your naked body," he admitted without an ounce of shame. "I'll get the water started."

"You do that. I'll get towels and soap."

Within minutes, the steam from the tub filled the small bathroom and Laci entered, her gaze going straight to Kane, who was already lounging in the antique tub like the lord of the manor and damn, did he look good. Seeing Kane naked like that was enough to wipe away even the worst memories and she didn't hesitate to join him. She gingerly stepped into the steaming water, placing her feet carefully between his legs, but as she braced herself on either side of the tub and began to lower herself, he caught her hips with his strong grip and she sucked in a tight breath as his teeth grazed her cheek.

"You have the world's most perfect ass," he told her almost reverently. "Makes me want to do bad things."

She closed her eyes, but a slow smile found her lips. "Yeah? What kind of bad things?"

"Dirty things," he growled. "The kind that good girls shouldn't know about."

She laughed and threw a coy look over her shoulder. "Who said I was a good girl?"

His brow climbed and he slowly spun her around, the water glistening on her thighs, lapping at her knees, as he said, "Oh? Are you saying you're a bad girl, Laci McCall?"

She bit her lip, watching as his gaze darkened at the tiny movement, and said breathlessly, "You have no idea how bad I can be."

The gauntlet had been thrown. Kane responded by burying his face between her folds, his tongue stabbing between her hot, needy flesh until she had to grip his shoulders or else fall. He was insatiable, groaning as he delved deeper, flicking her clit without mercy, driving her toward that single moment of indescribable pleasure until her knees trembled and she felt she might die from utter bliss as she shattered beneath his tongue, sagging against him as the waves washed over her, one crest after another.

Once she could breathe again, she lowered herself on shaky limbs into the water, sighing as complete happiness blanketed her every thought. Kane's chest at her back was a perfect cushion, although something was persistently poking her in the back. She wiggled against him and he groaned.

"That's not fair," he told her and she laughed, ignoring his poor condition to grab the soap. "You're going to leave me like this?" he bemoaned and she giggled. "Oh, you're a cruel woman. Just you wait…you have to get out of this tub eventually."

She laughed outright, ending on a sigh as she said, "I wish we could be like this forever. This is perfect."

"Yeah," he agreed softly, his cheek resting against her head. "It is."

A moment passed of easy but companionable silence and she wondered, if things had turned out differently between them—if Kane hadn't left when he did—would they have enjoyed this kind of happiness together or would they have fallen apart like so many other young couples, battered by fame and the pressure of celebrity life? It was impossible to know, but a part of her wondered if Kane hadn't made the right decision, even though it had hurt, because as he'd pointed out, things had worked out for them both in spite of their loss of each other. She thought of Kane's younger brother. "How's Rian these days?"

He chuckled and somehow his hands found her breasts, cupping them as if it was completely the thing to do while having a casual conversation in the bathtub together. "He's the same as ever. Always the cool guy, the guy all the girls seem to chase after."

She laughed at that. "I always thought he was a little goofy."

Kane chuckled. "I can't wait to tell him that. He

could use a little humble pie. He gets plenty of action, I can tell you that. No shortage of the honeys, if you know what I mean."

"Yes, I get it. So your little brother turned into a man-whore?" she joked.

"Completely. But in a gentlemanlike way," he said. His defense of his little brother warmed her heart, as it always did. "I'm kidding. He's a good man. Solid, dependable. I never worry about putting clients' lives in his hands."

"You've always looked out for Rian. I'm glad to see some things never change," she murmured, overwhelmed by the swell of emotion that followed. Kane, so gruff, yet so inherently good. How was it that some woman hadn't snatched him up? "There's no one special waiting for you?" she had to ask. He'd mentioned dating but hadn't gone into detail and she needed to know.

He squeezed her breasts from behind, drawing her more tightly to him as he answered, low and sweetly, against the shell of her ear. "The only person I ever considered special is filling my hands with her glorious tits." She sucked in an excited breath as fresh arousal hit her like a thunderbolt. His fingers found her nipples and lightly pinched, shooting tendrils of need and lust into her pelvis as he said, "In all the years since you and I were together, there's never been anyone who makes me feel as you do." His mouth traveled to her neck as he lightly nipped and sucked. "You are my drug, Laci McCall."

That was all she needed to hear. Turning, she found his lips and kissed him sweetly, deeply. Then she rose and graced him with a sultry look as she announced, "I've had enough of the bath. Time for bed."

And as she wrapped herself in a thick towel and walked to the bedroom, she smiled to herself as she heard him splashing to get out of the tub fast enough to send the contents all over the floor. Before she even heard the gurgle of the tub emptying, Kane was behind her. A quick glance over her bare shoulder revealed Kane, wet and dripping, eyes filled with hunger, his beautiful cock standing at full and eager attention as he reached for her, drawing her against him. "You know how to make a man forget everything he ever thought was true," he growled, the low timbre of his voice sending goose bumps rioting across her skin. "You are bad," he confirmed, the corners of his supple mouth twisting as his gaze fastened with hers.

She smiled, slow and sensuous, allowing her towel to drop to the floor, enjoying the sudden sound of Kane drawing a tight breath. "I'm not the innocent girl I used to be. Now, come here and let me show you a thing or two."

Before he could say another word, Laci was indeed showing him that country girls with sweet smiles could very well disguise a filthy and dirty mind.

Judging by the loud groans and the way Kane gasped her name…he didn't mind one little bit.

17

LACI STRETCHED AND YAWNED as the early-morning light filled the bedroom with warmth, and she sighed at the immediate bliss that filled her heart. Oh, the simple things… But just as her feet touched the hardwood floor, she heard a commotion out front and pulled on the first thing she could grab to go and investigate.

Of all the people she never expected to see…her manager was standing on the front porch, arguing with Kane something fierce and, by the look on Kane's face, Trent was dangerously close to flying head over keister off the porch. She flew down the stairs and edged her way past Kane to try to smooth things over before they escalated. "Trent, what are you doing here?" she exclaimed, placing a calming hand on Kane. "How'd you find me?"

"This is your manager?" Kane asked, his lip curling.

"Yes, I'm her manager and just who are you?"

Laci cut in before Kane could answer because she wasn't ready to put labels on what they'd shared. "Don't worry about him, Trent. What the Sam Hill are you doing here?"

"The bigger question is…what the hell are you doing playing country bumpkin when you've got a sold-out tour to finish, girlie?"

"Hey, don't talk to her like that," Kane interjected with a growl. "She's a grown woman and, technically, your boss, so a little respect is in order."

Trent's gaze narrowed and although he was shorter than Kane and definitely not quite as built, he didn't back down for a second, in fact going toe-to-toe with Kane as if he could take him. "I'm sorry, I seemed to have missed the connection… Just exactly who the hell are you? Because I've been managing this *woman*'s career for the past eight years and I've made her a superstar. In those eight years I've taken a country girl and turned her into a household name, what have you done for her?"

"You've run her into the ground for your own gain," Kane said, glaring hard enough to burn a hole through Trent's shirt. "That's what you've done for her. She had to run away from you just to get some rest."

Trent cut a mildly mocking glance at Laci as he said, "And that's what you've been doing here? Resting? Seems to me someone's forgotten how to tell the truth. I ain't dumb. I know what y'all been up to and that's fine by me, but there's work to be done. Ya hear? Work. That's what pays the bills and puts food on the table for your hardworking crew, like your friends Audrey and Simone. Remember them? Yeah, they been worried sick over you. How's that make you feel to know that while you've been gallivanting around, your friends have been twisted up with worry, thinking something terrible happened. Hell, it was all I could do to keep Simone from calling the authorities and putting out one of those alerts."

Laci's heart stopped and she felt like a toad for worrying her friends. She should've at least called Simone and Audrey to let them know that she was fine, but she'd needed a few days, or a week or two… Hell, she might've taken a whole month if Trent hadn't shown up, but reality was definitely pushing its way into her fantasy and it was time to pay the piper. "I'll go pack my things," she murmured unhappily.

Kane stopped her with a questioning look, but she couldn't leave the people who depended on her in the lurch. It just wasn't right and it wasn't how she was raised. Surely Kane could understand that, if nothing else. "It's just what I have to do."

"Bullshit," he disagreed hotly, shooting Trent a dark look. "This is on you. You've been pushing her too hard and now you're guilting her into coming back with you. If I hadn't promised I would keep my hands to myself, you'd be eating my fist for breakfast."

"Well, thank goodness for small favors," Trent drawled, then gestured to Laci, saying, "C'mon, girl, we got a plane to catch and a concert to put on. The public awaits."

"Laci…" Kane called after her, but she was already on the move. Her mind was racing and her heart was thumping in time with her guilty conscience. What had she been thinking to run off like that? It'd been the most irresponsible thing she'd ever done and she was embarrassed to have fallen apart so completely.

As she was throwing the scant amount of clothes she'd brought with her into her bag, Kane appeared in the doorway looking ready to break something. "You're seriously going to leave just like that? He snaps his fingers and you say how high? What the hell, Laci. He's not your daddy, he's your manager and he doesn't have the right to order you around like that."

"Kane, please. You don't understand. Trent Blackstone's been really good to me and I was terrible to run away without a word. I mean, I can't excuse my behavior. It was just plain rude and irresponsible considering how much I owe Trent."

"Did he do all this out of the goodness of his heart?" Kane asked, surprising her with the odd question.

"What do you mean?"

"I mean, did he catapult you into superstardom by the goodness of his heart? In other words…did you pay him to do a job?"

"Well, of course I paid him," she said, frowning. "What kind of question is that?"

"One that makes my point. He's not your friend or anything like that. He's getting paid pretty good to manage your life, but he's not the king…he's just a manager. You don't have to run off just because he said so."

"But the tour—"

"He could reschedule every single date if he had to. I know he could because I've seen it happen. He's pushing you hard because every sold-out venue is more money in his pocket. To be honest, I question the integrity of a man who would abuse his client like that."

"I'm not being abused," she said in a low tone. "And I don't appreciate what you're saying to me right now. You don't understand how the music business works, so don't try to insert your opinion where it's not wanted."

He laughed and she drew back in stung silence. "What's so funny?"

"Not funny so much as tragic. I'm the one concerned for your welfare and yet my opinion means nothing. The man tapping his toe and glancing at his watch is the man who is going to put you in the ground and probably find a way to make a buck off your funeral and yet, you're planning to leave with him. Unreal."

"You were right. This is why we would never work out, Kane," she said, fighting tears as she jerked her suitcase to the floor. "You automatically reject anything you don't agree with and then everyone else is the jerk. You don't understand my obligations and I don't have the time to try to explain them to you every time we disagree on this topic."

"This is damn ridiculous," he nearly shouted, clearly frustrated with her. "Don't go with that son of a bitch, please. Let's just talk this out. I can drive you to the airport later if that's what you need to do, but don't leave right now. Not like this."

"That would only delay the inevitable, Kane. You and I both knew this was coming. Please don't make it worse. Please tell Cora and Warren I love them."

"Tell them yourself. Or wait, there's no time on the tour for them, is there? Only for the legion of fans out there who want to own a lock of your hair or your dirty underpants that they bought off eBay for a couple hundred bucks."

"That's disgusting," she exclaimed, unable to believe Kane was sinking so low. "And we're done. Goodbye, Kane."

"Fine. Go. You're so damn stubborn you wouldn't admit the sky is blue even if blue was the only color in the rainbow. Have a nice life, Laci."

She climbed into the rented car and Trent wasted no time in leaving Kane and the Bradford ranch behind in a puff of dust.

For Laci, it felt as if she were leaving behind her heart.

KANE KICKED A rock from the porch and watched it sail across the yard to land in the grass with a muffled thud. She actually left with that man. He still couldn't believe it. And that panicked look on her face was more than he could stomach, which was crazy because she didn't want his concern. Trent—that was his name, right?—yeah, he just stood there, looking smug because he'd known that it didn't matter how much Kane blustered and threatened, she was going to leave with him. What kind of power did he have over Laci? Didn't seem right in the least. He went back into the house and immediately called Rian.

"Ri, I need you to do something for me," he said, going straight to the point.

"Hello to you, too. What's going on? Everything okay at the ranch?"

"Ranch is fine. It's Laci I'm worried about. She just left with her sleazy manager and I don't trust him farther than I can throw him. Can you run a background check?"

"Sure. What's his name?"

"Trent Blackstone."

"Got a DOB?"

"No. That's all I got. I can describe the asshole to you in case you need a visual."

"It's not ideal but sure, go for it."

"A little shorter than me, probably five foot eleven inches, slightly graying hair, looks to be in good shape for his age. Slightly pocked skin, as if he had a bad go of it when he was a kid."

"All right. What happened? You and Laci get into a fight or something?"

"No, everything was fine until he showed his ugly mug and it was like her whole world just imploded and she had to leave. I could tell she didn't want to go, but it seemed she had no choice in the matter."

"You think he's coercing her somehow?"

He shook his head, frustrated. "No, not exactly. Just pressured. He started spouting off about responsibility and whatnot and she caved like a wet napkin stretched over a glass, but she wasn't ready to go back. In fact, I was trying to get her to see that she was being run into the ground by this guy right when he showed up."

"How'd he know where to find her? She call him?"

"No. Her cell's been turned off the whole time. I never saw her once on the phone to anyone. I got the impression she didn't want anyone finding her just yet because she wasn't ready."

"Hold on, let me check something." There was a pause and then Rian returned, saying, "He may have just checked TMZ. There's a picture of you and her at the festival."

"Damn vultures. I knew going to that festival would bite us in the ass. I warned her that it wasn't a good idea but she had to have a candied apple."

"Yeah, well, hopefully that apple was worth it. Now, there's all sorts of speculation about who Laci's 'mystery man' is. I'm surprised reporters haven't been banging down the door already."

"They can go ahead and try. Shotgun still works as an effective no-trespassing message."

"Don't go shooting people," Rian grumbled. "That's all we need."

"Don't worry about me—you just see what you can dig up on that loser manager of hers."

"Well, are you sure you want to put your nose in her business? Might not go over very well. Laci's a strong woman. I doubt this guy is pushing her around."

"You didn't see her around him," Kane grumbled, still a little baffled by what he'd just witnessed. "I don't know, maybe you're right. She's gonna be pissed as hell if I poke around in her business, but something doesn't sit right and I can't just let it slide because I might get yelled at."

"All right, you're the boss. I'll poke around and see what pops out." Rian paused a beat, then said, "So, I take it hanging out with Laci…it's been good?"

"Yeah, it's been pretty good. I mean, we've had our moments, but—" Kane stopped, flustered, not quite sure how to talk about his feelings for Laci. Not even with his own brother because he wasn't sure of his own mind and heart. Well, that wasn't entirely accurate. His heart and mind were at opposite sides of the situation, both urging him to do completely divergent things. His heart wanted Laci. Had never stopped wanting Laci. But his mind freaked the hell out at the very idea because it was a doomed love affair from the start. Only a glutton for punishment would chase after something that they knew wasn't going anywhere. He scrubbed at his head with his free hand, agitated, and finally said, "Listen, I just want to make sure she's safe. After that…I don't have any answers."

"You don't have to have all the answers all the time," Rian said, surprising him. "Look, it's your business, but maybe it's time to admit that Laci is still under your skin and it's time to figure out what that means."

"It means there's no room in her life for me," he barked, ready for Rian to just do as he asked and stop playing armchair shrink. "Call me when you've got something."

Rian barked back, "Fine, you pigheaded fool. I'll call. In the meantime, try to do some soul-searching to rattle that pea brain of yours."

Fabulous. Love advice from his little brother—a man who was so gun-shy about commitment, he'd never kept a girlfriend longer than six months—yeah, that was rich.

He hung up, and because he couldn't sit around all

day waiting for the phone to ring, went back outside to do some repairs on the fence line. At least if his hands were occupied, his brain would settle down for just a minute.

Or at least, he hoped.

"DID YOU ENJOY your little impromptu freak-out?" Trent asked with a subtle curl of scorn in his tone that caused Laci to frown. They were settled into the plane, getting ready for takeoff and now Trent was feeling chatty apparently. "I had to call in a few favors to find you in that Podunk town. Who's ever heard of Woodsville, Kentucky? I'm surprised it's even on a map. Thank goodness for GPS on a cell phone."

Laci remained silent, choosing instead to gaze out the window. Everything felt wrong. Maybe she shouldn't have let Trent panic her like that. She could still see Kane's expression of shock when she chose Trent over him, but honestly, it wasn't her choosing Trent over Kane, it was all the people who depended on her for their livelihood that propelled her to action. She couldn't let them down. "I'm sorry. I was going to call," she murmured, leaning against the window frame, trailing her finger against the hard plastic shutter. "I just wanted a few days of peace and quiet. I didn't mean to worry anyone."

"Yeah, well, you did," Trent said. "Worried me sick. You know this is going to take a bite out of your payday. Losing out on gigs…that's just bad business. You don't want to gain a reputation for being a flighty no-show because then you won't get booked again. Promoters have long memories, girl. Do you hear me? Long memories. And it's going to take a while to live this one down."

"I said I was sorry," she said, some of her fire returning. "Enough already."

Trent smiled thinly. "Look at you—all country sass. Just remember what side your bread is buttered."

"How could I forget when you're constantly reminding me?" she returned, not caring that she was being sassy and unaccountably rude to the man who'd made her a star. She could practically hear her daddy's voice chastising her, but she was tired, grouchy and already missing Kane, so her tongue was a little loose. As soon as they landed, she needed to call him and make sure he knew that she wasn't running away from him, that she still wanted to see him. "I want tickets made available to Kane Dalton for the show tomorrow," she told Trent, not asking but telling.

"And who is this Kane Dalton, exactly?"

She hesitated, irritated that Trent was even questioning. Maybe Kane was right and Trent had forgotten which side *his* bread was buttered. "Don't worry about who he is. Just have the tickets ready."

"Sure thing, sugar. Just curious, is all. It's my job to look out for your welfare, you know. Your daddy made me promise with his dying breath that I would always do what was best for you and I aim to keep that promise, even if you're being a right pill about it."

She recognized manipulation when she saw it, but it was still hard to avoid falling into it when her daddy was involved because she knew it was true. Her daddy had thought Trent Blackstone was the be-all and end-all for her career and, she supposed, he'd been right, to a point, but she suspected that if he'd lived and could see how Trent was running her into the ground, he'd have something to say about that.

"So what favors exactly did you call in to find me?" she asked, curious.

"Does it matter?" he answered with a patronizing smile. He patted her leg and said, "You just focus on warming up that voice. Kelly Clarkson was the last country artist to sell out this venue and we don't want to appear as if you can't do the same. You have to show your fans that you're ready to perform, and nothing matters but giving the fans what they want."

"What about what I want?" she muttered, but when Trent cut her a short look, she shook her head and returned her gaze to the view. She didn't want to be on a plane, she didn't want to be sitting next to Trent. She wanted…a small farmhouse with a wraparound porch, the smell of cattle and horses on the breeze, and Kane touching every inch of her body with his hands and mouth. A small, sad sigh escaped and that probably would've been the end of it, but Trent wanted his pound of flesh and started berating her.

"I can't believe what a pouty little girl you're turning into, Laci McCall. You're a damn star. Start acting like one. Playing house in the country isn't what you signed up for, remember? If that's all you wanted, you signed up with the wrong man, because I represent talented people with ambition. What happened to that hungry, driven girl with her eye on the prize? You done bumped your head if you think that acting the way you've been acting is going to get anywhere but the bottom faster than you can blink. To be frank, I almost washed my hands of you the minute you ran off. You're a grown-ass woman. Why am I chasing after you like a kid lost at the county fair? I haven't the faintest."

"Because I make you a lot of money," Laci answered with a yawn. "Leave me alone, Trent. You aren't the only manager out there. If you're not happy with me… you know where the door is."

He barked an ugly, incredulous laugh. "Girl, you're just talking out of your pretty ass. Did your country boy screw your brains out? Think, girl! Think what you're saying and check yourself before you wreck yourself. I'll let that one slide on account of you being tired and all, but watch yourself."

Laci cast a dark glower Trent's way but remained silent. She wasn't going to spend the entire plane ride bickering with her manager. But as she returned her gaze to the window, she knew without a doubt it was time to get new management. Kane was right; this guy didn't have her best interests at heart and probably never had. However, for the sake of a peaceful plane ride, Laci kept that decision to herself. That uncomfortable conversation could wait.

She closed her eyes and dreamed of Kane.

18

IN SPITE OF her lack of enthusiasm to get back onstage right away, Laci was happy to see Audrey and Simone, who were clearly very happy to see her, as well.

"Girl, did you have a mental breakdown or something? Why did you leave the hospital?" Audrey asked once they were on the tour bus in her private section. "Man, you should've seen Trent. I thought he was going to pop a vein."

"I'm sorry to have worried you," Laci said. She tried to come up with an explanation for her behavior, if only to assuage the pinch to her conscience for worrying her team. "When Trent told me he had rebooked the tour, I just lost it. I was so tired, so mentally undone, that I couldn't fathom getting back on that stage. If he had even given me a week to recover, I think I could've sucked it up and carried on, but I just broke when he said that."

Audrey nodded with understanding, saying with an angry glint in her eye, "That no-good rat. I told him you were exhausted but he doesn't listen. He threatened to fire Simone when he found out you were gone."

"What?"

Simone nodded, confirming Audrey's statement. "But he's a blowhard. I didn't take him serious. I knew once you came back you'd fix it. We were just worried you weren't coming back, not that we'd blame you. Trent's been a bit of a Nazi with your scheduling. Trust me, we're tired, too." Simone lifted her fingers, showing off the cuts and bruises from sewing countless sequins after every show. "If I see another sequin, I'm about to run off, myself. Have you considered maybe jeans and a T-shirt?" she joked half-seriously.

Laci chuckled ruefully, though the idea held merit. She liked the idea of dressing things down, but Trent wouldn't hear of it. He always said people paid top dollar to see a star, not a honky-tonk weekend wannabe. "Let's modify the costuming a bit. I always feel like a disco ball anyway with all those sequins," she suggested to Simone, who, judging by her relieved smile, agreed with the idea.

"So, are you going to tell us where you went?" Audrey asked. Laci's smile was wistful as she pictured the Bradford ranch, and a warm, happy feeling followed that was hard to hide. Audrey whistled low and said, "Okay, now I totally need details, girl. Dish!"

"Okay, okay, I don't usually kiss and tell, but…I went back to a place I used to spend my summers at called Bradford ranch. The older couple who live there were like grandparents to me and I thought I could use a little country air to detox and get back to my roots. But when

I got there, they were gone, and watching over the place was…you're not going to believe this…my first love."

Simone's eyes bugged and she gasped. "Are you kidding me? Did you just step out of the pages of a Nicholas Sparks book? Who does that happen to? That's crazy."

"It's only a Nicholas Sparks book if the love of her life died in some crazy farming accident while she was there," Audrey quipped, and they all giggled. "Okay, in all seriousness…what happened? Did you connect? Relive old times? Where is he now?"

"Whoa, whoa, too many questions at once," Laci said, holding up her hands. "The truth is, things were going really good until Trent showed up and I felt obligated to come back."

"Why didn't he just come with you?" Simone asked, confused.

"Because that's not how Kane Dalton rolls," Laci answered drily, but felt she ought to add, "However, I didn't give him much opportunity to tag along. I just, sort of, panicked and left with Trent. I don't know. It was like reality had intruded on my little fantasy and I didn't know how to reconcile the two. I think if I'd been smart, I would've just talked it out with him, but… lately, I've been doing all sorts of things that fall in the 'not smart' category."

"Don't be so hard on yourself," Simone admonished, instantly making Laci feel marginally better. "Invite him to the show. Does he like your music?"

"Aside from my daddy, he was my biggest fan when we were kids," Laci answered, nodding. "But so much has changed. He's already said he's not cut out to follow me around and I understand that. I just wish things were different. I think, no…I know, that I never stopped loving him. He's the sexiest, most handsome man I've ever laid eyes on and that body—" she fanned herself "—you can't even imagine! Thank God there were chores to be done. Otherwise, I might not be able to walk still."

Audrey and Simone both *awwwwwed* and crowded her with fierce hugs before Audrey decided, "Well, it's settled then, you have to get him here. Just because I'm single and dateless doesn't mean you have to be, especially when your man—who just happens to be your soul mate, right?—is just waiting for you to claim him."

"I wouldn't say he's waiting on me," Laci said with a sinking heart. "Kane is the kind of man who doesn't pine for the attentions of a woman. Not even me. He's not coming after me. Besides, he's busy with the ranch, he can't just pick up and leave. Plus, I wouldn't want him to. He's helping out the Bradfords when they need it the most and that's exactly what he should be doing. I just wish things were different for everyone."

Both women seemed to understand and gave Laci a beat of silence before Simone said, "Well, if the show must go on, we'd better take a look at your costume and see what needs changing. You up for it?"

Laci sighed. "Yeah, though I should warn you, I've been doing nothing but eating pie and potatoes, so I'm probably fatter than a summer tick on a whitetail right now."

"I'm sure I can make it work, don't you worry," Simone said, waving away Laci's concern. "Besides, a man likes a little meat on his woman's bones, right?"

Laci grinned, immediately thinking of the way Kane worshipped her curves, his hands roaming her hips and his tongue tracing each lush valley, and she shivered with a weighty exhale. "I miss him already," she murmured and the girls dissolved into envious laughter.

Kane...I wish you were here.

KANE HAD EXPECTED a phone call, but since Laci had hightailed it out of there with that jerk-off manager of hers, it'd been radio silence. He didn't know her cell phone number—not that he would call—but he supposed his ego had been bruised that she'd just split and apparently left him behind.

What had he expected? He knew she was out there singing her tail off again. He'd broken down and scoured the internet for news of her concert in Texas and even caught a few screenshots fans had posted. She looked amazing—no, better than amazing, downright sizzling—and then he'd felt worse off than before. Time to stop moping around for a woman who had never truly been his. They'd been playing around, reliving old times, not building for a future. He got that. But damn, if it didn't hurt just the same.

He rubbed at his chest as if he could massage out the phantom pain digging right below his rib cage and went to the front porch to watch the last of the light die out on the horizon. He had to admit the ranch wasn't so bad. Hell, even Woodsville wasn't the hellhole he'd remembered it to be. There was a quiet charm to the old town, and the ranch soothed his soul in a way that he hadn't expected. He liked the simplicity of tending to the animals, getting the chores done and sitting down to a meal that stuck to his ribs. Although since Laci had split, he'd just made a big pot of beans and rice, which he shoved down his throat with a tortilla he warmed up on the stove and slathered with butter. Still, he hadn't realized how much he'd needed a little downtime until he'd been forced to get some by circumstance.

Just as the last rays of light sank into the horizon, gulped by the greedy landscape, the old phone in the house rang shrilly, cutting the serene quiet and interrupting the building cricket cacophony.

Kane caught the ringing phone just before it went to the answering machine, hoping it was Laci. But when it was Warren, he immediately tensed for fear of bad news.

"Everything okay?" he asked.

"Not so good, boy," Warren admitted, his voice watery. "Not so good at all."

Kane checked his watch, concerned. "It's pretty late out there. Cora okay?"

"She's gone," Warren said, his voice breaking. "My girl is gone. She just couldn't take no more and slipped away when I went to get some coffee. I think she knew, too, because she kept pestering me to go eat something when I wouldn't leave her side. And then, dadgum it, the minute I do—" he drew a sad, shaky breath "—she left me behind."

Stunned, Kane's butt found the nearest chair. "Oh, man" was all he could say because the news hit him that hard. He didn't know how to follow it up because his heart was breaking alongside Warren's. "I'm…I'm out of words," he said, his voice choking. "What happened?"

"The treatment was too late. The cancer was too spread out, the doc said. She tried to tell me, but I wouldn't listen. Cora…she's a tough one but not tougher than the Big C, you know?"

"Yeah, I know. Man, I can't…" He wiped at his eyes, unable to believe Cora was gone. That feisty, yet interminably sweet, woman had earned a spot in his heart the minute she'd made it her mission to "fatten him up" all those years ago. She'd seen his thin arms and hungry eyes and she'd stuffed him full of love in the form of good old-fashioned cooking.

God bless it! More tears followed as he listened to Warren share the details of Cora's last days and, when it was all said and done, Kane knew that perhaps it'd been a blessing she'd gone in her sleep. Cora deserved a peaceful exit, not some drawn-out painful end. "What's the plan, you coming home soon, then?" he asked, wiping his nose and trying to dry his eyes with his shirtsleeve.

"I've got details to deal with here and then I'm having Cora brought home for a proper funeral. She'd want it that way. Is Laci still there?"

A lump formed in his throat and Kane answered stiffly, "She left. Her manager came and collected her last week. Haven't heard from her since."

"Well, you go find her. Cora would've wanted her at the funeral. I don't care what you have to do to get her there."

"Yes, sir." He made the commitment, but frankly, he

wasn't sure he wanted to see Laci. It felt right stingy of him, but he was double hurting now that Cora was gone, and maybe if Laci hadn't been in such an all-fired hurry to leave, she would've been here to get the news herself. But he couldn't refuse Warren and said dutifully, "I'll see what I can do."

"Good boy," Warren said in a tired voice. "I'll be in touch in a few days."

Warren clicked off and Kane sat staring at the floor for a long moment. He should've taken the time to visit more often. The random phone calls weren't enough. Guilt for not squeezing more time in with the people who mattered in his life kicked him swiftly in the ass, but there was no fixing what had been done, as Cora used to tell him. Now he had to find a way to get a hold of Laci.

He picked up his cell and called Rian.

Rian answered with an "I was just about to call you" and Kane broke in to deliver the bad news. Rian, just as stunned, took a long moment to recover. "Shit," he muttered, his voice breaking. "I had a feeling this was going to go this way."

"Yeah, I think in the back of my mind, I did, too, but I was hoping for something different. I thought maybe this treatment… I don't know, I guess I was hoping for a miracle."

"Me, too."

Kane relayed Warren's request and then also shared how conflicted he was about it. "Am I being a selfish prick?" he asked his brother.

"Naw, you're just hurting, man. That's all. But I think I can help you there. I have Laci's number."

"What?"

"Yeah, I figured it might be a good idea to hold on to it. You never know when it might come in handy that you know a country-music star."

He wasn't sure how well it sat with him that Rian had been holding on to Laci's number, but he had bigger fish to fry. "Give it to me," he grumbled, and his cell phone chimed as the contact came through. "Funeral is sometime next week. Warren is busy taking care of the details of, you know, bringing her home."

"God, that's rough. Okay, I'll clear my schedule." He paused a beat, then asked, "You want me to call Laci and tell her the news?"

Kane scowled. Hell no. If the news would come from anyone, it would come from him. "I got this. You just handle your end. Have you found anything on that manager of hers?"

"Not really. I mean, aside from the fact that he's a dick. Not well liked in certain circles, but he seems to have a knack for turning out stars."

That wasn't the news he'd been hoping for, but then, what had he expected Rian to find? That the guy was a wanted terrorist, living under an assumed name? "All right. Keep looking, you never know what might pop up. Hell, maybe he cheats on his taxes or something."

Rian chuckled ruefully. "Yeah, okay. I'll see you in a few days."

Kane clicked off and he stared at the text message with Laci's contact number. He supposed he ought to keep it short and sweet. Maybe he'd just send a text and let her decide whether or not she wanted to call back. But sending a text for something so personal seemed chickenshit, so in the end, he just punched in the numbers and held his breath.

One ring, two rings, three rings—voice mail.

Well, hell. He didn't want to leave that kind of message, either, so he clicked off. He'd try again later.

He yawned and pocketed his phone before turning off the lights in the house and climbing into bed.

The only good thing about working his ass off was that sleep came easily even if his brain didn't want to shut off.

He just didn't have a choice.

Thank God for small favors.

19

THE FOLLOWING DAY they were somewhere between Tulsa and New Mexico when Trent picked up Laci's silently vibrating cell phone and waited for the call to go to voice mail. He didn't recognize the number and it wasn't in Laci's contacts, but his gut told him it was that hulking country guy who didn't need to be calling and pestering his number one star.

Laci, sacked out in the private section of the tour bus, had put on one helluva show last night and the ticket sales were enough to make him forgive Laci for her momentary lapse in reason. But this—he stared at the cell phone with distaste—was enough to bring back bad memories. Without hesitation, he listened to the voice mail, curling his lip when he heard that man's voice.

"Laci, this is Kane... Call me when you get the chance. It's important."

Hmm...no loving send-off, just a curt message left behind. What could be more important than keeping his country angel focused and on-target? Trent didn't think anything was more important than that. In a deliberate action, he deleted the voice mail as well as the missed-call signal. His job was to keep Laci focused on the future, not looking back to the past. He began to return the phone to where he found it, but then he reconsidered and pocketed it instead. Best way to keep his star focused was to remove distractions.

LACI AWOKE AND rubbed bleary eyes as she attempted to focus her vision. Her head was splitting and every muscle ached. She needed a good, deep massage and a handful of aspirin with her morning coffee.

She rolled to her side to grab her phone and realized she'd left it in the front of the bus last night. She'd been so exhausted, she hadn't even taken the time to clean the makeup from her face, and normally she never slept with makeup on because it clogged her pores.

She slowly climbed from her bed and stumbled to the private bathroom to rinse her face. Staring into the small mirror, she saw unhappiness staring back at her. She needed to call Kane. Part of her was ashamed by how she'd run out on him, moving on autopilot instead of using her brain to think things through, but then Trent knew how to get the right reaction out of her, too. She shook her head, bogged down by the weight of her own life.

She braced herself on her elbows against the counter and stretched her back, wincing as her muscles screamed and her back ached. She felt a hundred years old today. Straightening slowly, she exited the bathroom and went in search of her phone, but Trent intercepted her with a glass of freshly squeezed orange juice and a bran muffin, packed with protein, no doubt, which would taste like cardboard but serve as the necessary fuel for the day.

"Thanks." She accepted the muffin and took a bite, grimacing. Yep. Cardboard. Nothing like Cora's muffins, which were loaded with butter and eggs, and love. She chewed dutifully and washed the muffin down with a swallow of orange juice. Well, at least the juice was good. "Have you seen my phone?"

Trent shook his head. "No, but I'm sure it's around here somewhere. Is there someone you need to call? I can do it for you."

She hesitated, not sure if she wanted to rely on Trent any more than she already did, particularly when she was considering letting him go, but her head hurt and she didn't want to add more stress to the day, so she just said, "It's not important. I'll take care of it later."

"Excellent," he said briskly with an efficient smile as he continued without missing a beat, "because you have a full day on the schedule. You have an interview with *Country Talk* magazine as well as a photo shoot for the December cover of *Cosmopolitan*, so let's get our head in the game. I want you to talk up the new album, give some private insight to the meaning of a song— people love that—but make sure you leave some mystery, too. An overexposed star is a star whose fame is waning. Got that?"

She nodded wearily, too tired to scowl or argue with him. "What time does everything start?"

"I have hair and makeup scheduled in one hour, so

you'd better scoot and get showered up. Go on, girl, get the lead out. Time's a-wasting."

Oh, shut up. She did manage a faint scowl this time, but it was lost on Trent. He was already moving on, heading to the front of the bus to give the driver their next destination.

A part of her insisted that she find a phone and call Kane, but the other part of her, likely the part that was still reluctant to go against Trent, was telling her to get her butt in the shower. It was a big deal to land the *Cosmo* cover. Country singers weren't always the ones sought after for that iconic cover, but as Trent liked to point out, she had the goods. Trent made sure she was made up for the public eye so she always looked radiant and beautiful, but truthfully, she'd enjoyed the fact that when Kane had looked at her, no matter if she'd just woken up and her hair was standing on end, or if she'd spent time on her hair and makeup, she knew he liked what he saw. No, more than liked—he'd loved it. Tears sprang to her eyes and she dashed them away, knowing she didn't have time to cry. The world didn't wait for a forlorn heart to mend—or to make up its mind.

She'd call Kane tonight, no matter what.

RIAN ARRIVED AT the Bradford ranch two days after Warren had returned. The air in the ranch house was stoic, as if no one dared to break down because if one fell to tears, they'd end up a sobbing mess and there was work to be done.

"How's Warren doing?" Rian asked once they were alone. Rian and Kane had headed for the barn to saddle up the horses to check the fence line where Kane had mended it a week prior.

"As good as can be expected, I suppose," Kane answered as he mounted Amelia, and Rian took Dancer. "He's real quiet, but then Warren's never been a man of many words. What can he say? She's gone and nothing's bringing her back."

"True. I just feel terrible for the old guy. I don't even know how he's going to function without Cora around. You know, Cora ran this ranch even if he did the heavy lifting. She paid the bills, the taxes, kept the house from falling down around their ears...and Warren's not up to learning a whole new set of skills."

"I know," Kane said grimly. Rian wasn't voicing anything he didn't already know. "But we knew sooner or later this day would come. It's just here now. But Warren's not going to let anyone come in and help him. His pride is thicker than molasses in winter."

"I been thinking...what if we offered to buy the ranch—me and you—and just kept Warren on to manage the operations?"

The idea had merit, but Warren wouldn't sell. Not even to him and Rian. "I wish that were the answer, but you know Warren's not going to let go of the ranch. Not until the good Lord takes him. That's the only way it's going to happen."

"Aw, hell, this ain't gonna work. We live in LA. We can't move our base of operations to Woodsville, Kentucky, to make sure Warren ain't killing himself here on the ranch." Just like Kane, when Rian was frustrated, the Southern came out in him, revealing his Kentucky roots. "This is a right pickle. Talk about being between a rock and a hard place."

Kane agreed, adding almost hopelessly, "Maybe I could convince Warren to take on a ranch hand…"

"Are you kidding? He wouldn't even let anyone take over temporarily while he took Cora for that stupid treatment. He ain't gonna let no stranger come in and help out now."

Kane swore under his breath because Rian was right. They rode in silence for a long while then Rian said, "You heard from Laci?"

"Nope."

"Did you leave a message with that number I gave you?"

"Yep."

"Are you sure she got the message? I know Laci wouldn't have kept radio silence if she knew about Cora. She loved the old gal like we all did."

Kane shot Rian a quelling look. He didn't want to talk about Laci. "It is what it is. I left a message. She hasn't called back. Can't get more clearer than that."

Rian looked confused. "I don't understand… Laci would never—"

"You're confusing what you knew of Laci when she was a kid with the woman she is now—they ain't the same. Trust me."

"I guess you're right, but I still can't believe she'd ignore a call like that. I mean, not even a text message back?"

"Nothing," Kane answered, trying not to let his anger get the best of him. He'd been damn surprised that Laci hadn't lifted a finger to call him since she'd bolted, but then, what had he expected? They'd shared some good times and now it was time for everyone to get back to reality, a reality that apparently didn't include him, and it stung. "Laci McCall is not the center of the universe. We got bigger problems to solve than whether or not Laci is going to remember who was there before she got famous."

Rian was quiet for a minute and Kane thought, *Good, he's dropping the subject*, but no such luck. "I don't buy it. She didn't get the message, Kane. Try again. You can't just send a single message and leave it at that. Sometimes technology eats messages, you know that. Remember that time I texted you to get beer and you came back from the store empty-handed?"

"This isn't like that," Kane retorted, shaking his head. "C'mon now, we got bigger stuff to figure out." He did a double take at his brother. "And why are you so hell-bent on me and Laci mending fences? You got a stake in this or something?"

"Yeah, actually, I do," Rian snapped. "It doesn't take a rocket scientist to see that you're still in love with the woman. And I have a feeling that if you don't chase after her, you're gonna regret it for the rest of your life and, frankly, I don't have time to babysit your sulking, crybaby ass just because you're too chickenshit to just lay it all on the line and tell her how you feel."

"Feeling your oats today, boy?"

"I'm not a boy," Rian growled as Dancer shied away from Amelia, reacting to the tension in her rider. "That's your problem, Kane. You're too bullheaded for your own damn good. You can't recognize when you need to listen to someone else."

"I'm not gonna chase after her like some lovelorn kid. I wouldn't do it when I was seventeen and I sure as hell don't see myself doing it now. She knows where to find me. At least for the next week. After that…she's out of luck."

Rian shook his head in disgust and spurred Dancer to a canter to put some space between him and Kane, which was probably a good thing. Amelia was getting happy feet and when she did that, she got skittish. He'd taken more than one spill on Amelia in his youth.

Was he being too stubborn? What else was he supposed to do? Pack up and drag the woman back to Woodsville so she could pay her respects to a woman who'd been like a grandmother to her? And what if that pushy manager got in the way again? He couldn't promise he wouldn't give that man a taste of pure country retribution in the form of his fist. *Just give her another call*, a voice urged, and he wavered. Rian was right, Laci would've called back if she'd known it was about Cora. Maybe he should've been more specific in his message. The funeral was in two days. He had to at least try.

If he didn't, Cora was likely to haunt his ever-loving ass for the rest of his days.

And he couldn't handle that idea at all.

20

THE WEEK PASSED in a blur, so much so that Laci didn't know which end was up any longer, but as Sunday arrived, she was thankful for the reprieve. Today was the day she was going to try to call Kane. Her stomach pitched and rolled at the prospect because she didn't know what to expect. She knew she had to try to explain, to try to get Kane to understand why she'd left that day. But the reality was, if she didn't understand, herself, why she'd left, how could she explain to somebody who didn't understand the lifestyle she lived? Perhaps that's why she hadn't been able to make the call yet. Either way, she wasn't going to sit on her hands any longer. Kane deserved some kind of answer.

"Trent, have you seen my phone? I seem to keep misplacing it." She began lifting papers from tabletops in search of her missing smartphone, getting frustrated by the fact that it seemed to have grown legs. "I can't understand why this phone keeps disappearing. Maybe I need a bell attached to it."

"Are you sure you should be on the phone right now? You ought to be resting your voice. You sounded a little hoarse at the last interview," Trent said. "Maybe you need a little tea with whiskey and lemon."

"I don't want to rest, I want my phone," she said, irritated. "Do you know where it is or not?"

Trent sounded bored as he flipped through the newspaper. "Nothing worse than a woman who thinks she knows her own mind. You need sleep. Now go on and get some shut-eye. I don't want to hear about how tired you are if you won't get some rest when you're able."

Red-hot anger washed through Laci like a flash flood barreling through a dusty canyon and she couldn't stop her mouth from snarling as she said, "Don't talk to me like I'm some kind of idiot. I pay your bills, not the other way around. Try to remember that."

"Don't get your dander up, girl. I was just trying to help. Who are you all fired up to talk to anyway?" he grumbled, folding the paper and standing. "If you just tell me what you need, I'll see to it that you get it."

But she didn't believe him. She didn't know why she was suddenly so suspicious of Trent, but it was as if her internal monitor was beeping like crazy and it was hard to shut it off. "I don't think that's any of your business," she returned coolly. Her patience with Trent was at an all-time low. She no longer saw him as the man with the key to her dreams but rather the gatekeeper preventing her from her own life. "It's not your job to manage who I talk to. If you have my phone, give it to me now."

"You're all filled with piss and vinegar today, aren't you? Calm down, your phone is right here."

Trent reached into his pocket and handed her the cell phone. "I found it underneath a bunch of costuming. You must've dropped it when you were changing. I was going to give it back to you after you'd had some rest."

She accepted the phone and although his explanation seemed plausible enough, she wondered if her phone had not been misplaced at all but deliberately hidden. Every time she'd asked for it, Trent had distracted her with something else. She checked her missed calls and her heart sank a little when she didn't see any unknown numbers in the missed-call list. Disappointment sharpened her voice even further as she said, "Keep your hands off my phone. This is personal property, and don't forget it."

She disappeared into her bedroom and closed the door, happy to shut him out if at least for the moment. Laci sank onto the bed, heartsick and angry at the same time. Why hadn't Kane called? It's true she hadn't left her number, but Kane had ways of finding information. If he'd wanted to find her, he would have. But the absence of any missed calls told her he hadn't been interested in finding her at all. Apparently, what she'd thought they'd shared at the ranch had been a passing diversion for him. Just because two people had sexual chemistry didn't mean they were meant to be together. It was a tough lesson, but what could she do? She supposed she could call him, but her pride balked at that. There was no way she was going to chase after him if he had no interest in being with her.

But how else was she going to get news about Cora? Laci chewed her bottom lip, conflicted. Maybe she'd just have to bite the bullet to find out how Cora was doing. Yes, that's what she would have to do. If Kane didn't want her, that was fine, but she wasn't going to let her issues with him get in the way of her love for Cora. She quickly dialed the Bradford ranch. And was surprised when not Kane but Rian answered the phone.

"Rian? Is that you?"

Rian, just as surprised, exclaimed, "Laci? Oh man, am I glad to hear your voice. Where are you? Please tell me you're close."

She frowned in confusion. "I'm in Oklahoma, I think. Why? What's going on?" A cold chill chased her spine. "Please tell me Cora is okay. Why are you there? Is it Kane? Is Kane okay?"

"Did you get Kane's message?"

"What message? No, I didn't get a message or a missed call from Kane. Are you saying that he tried to call me?" Laci couldn't stop the hope in her voice even though she was scared at what her intuition was telling her was coming. "I swear to you I didn't get any message. What's going on?" The heaviness in Rian's voice confirmed her fear that Cora was gone. "No...please tell me that Cora's okay," she pleaded, tears springing to her eyes.

"She died last week. Her poor old body couldn't handle those treatments any longer. Warren had her brought back so that she could be buried in her hometown. The funeral is today," he said mournfully. "I was hoping that you were gonna tell me you were on your way and almost here. But if you're in Oklahoma...there's no way you're going to make it in time."

Her heart broke into a million tiny pieces, shattering and splintering as the reality that Cora was gone hit her with a force of a collapsing building. "She's really gone? Oh God, please tell me that's not true. I never got to say goodbye. I never got to tell her how much I love her."

"Kane tried to call you. Twice. He's a real mess—he thinks you don't care."

"But I do care, I care a lot. I just didn't know. Damn you, Trent!" She knew it was Trent who'd waylaid those messages. She knew in her heart as well as she knew anything to be true. "If I'd known, nothing would've stopped me from being there. What time is the funeral? Maybe I can hop a plane and get there on time."

"You can try, but I'm not holding out hope. The funeral's at four o'clock today."

"I'm going to try. You tell Kane I'm coming." She scrubbed the tears from her eyes, too angry to cry right now. She would have to mourn Cora later. Right now she had to find a way to get to Kentucky before that funeral. Rian gave her the details and then she hung up and started yelling for Trent. First things first, Trent had to go.

"What's all the racket?" Trent asked as Laci came screaming out of her bedroom. "Have you lost your mind? What are you hollering about?"

"You slimy bastard. You kept my phone so that I wouldn't see that Kane was calling me. Why would you do that?"

Trent's expression hardened and he didn't appear the least bit remorseful; if anything, he seemed flippant, as if he'd do it again if he could and that just boiled her blood. "And what if I did? I only did it to keep you focused. You've been a loose cannon lately. Running off, hiding in the country, playing house with some hillbilly while the rest of us think you're off dead somewhere. Stop acting so selfish and think of how your actions are affecting others."

"Oh no you don't," she said, so angry her voice shook. "Don't you dare throw my responsibilities in my face ever again. I never would've run if you hadn't tried to work me into the grave with that insane schedule you booked. I told you over and over I needed a break but you didn't listen. What else was I supposed to do? And this isn't about me. This is about you, hijacking my personal property when you had no right to do so."

"That's where you're wrong," he said, stabbing a finger her way. "You represent an investment of time and money on my part and I wasn't about to let some guy come in and ruin what I built over the last eight years. If you like your life, you have *me* to thank, you ungrateful bitch."

A month ago, Laci would've crumpled at Trent's hot words but not today. Today was about making things right when they'd gone terribly wrong. "If you like *your* life, you can thank *me*, you overbearing asshole. If it weren't for me, you, you wouldn't have the lifestyle you hold so dear."

"Women like you are a dime a dozen. I could walk down the streets of Nashville and pick up the first cute blonde with a semidecent voice singing on the street for quarters and dimes and probably get a more well-mannered client than you."

"You don't have the right to police my phone calls," she shouted. "You're my manager, not my lord and master. You kept a very important phone call from me and because of you I'm going to miss the funeral of someone I love very much. And for that, I can't forgive you."

Trent narrowed his stare. "And what's that supposed to mean?" He looked incredulous. "You trying to fire me, girl?"

"There's no trying about it—we're through. You stepped over the line and this is me putting my foot in your ass. Get off my bus."

Trent laughed. "I ain't going nowhere. This is my bus. If you want off, you can get off right now."

She stared hard. "If that's what it takes, that's what'll happen. I'm not spending another ten seconds in the same space as you."

"Careful, some words you can't take back. Think about what you're saying."

"Oh, I know exactly what I'm saying. And I stand by every word. I used to think that I had to do and say everything you told me to because you were the smart one in this relationship, you were the one who knew the business. But I don't need you anymore. You abused the power that I gave you and frankly, I don't even like you. I never have. And no one else likes you, either, so get the hell out of my life."

"Oh, you're going to regret this. And when you come crawling back on your hands and knees, I'm going to have to think long and hard before taking you back."

It was Laci's turn to laugh. "As if that's ever going to happen. I'd rather go back to playing in small honky-tonks with twenty people in the audience than spend another minute under your thumb just to sell out venues. I'm done."

She grabbed her purse and walked up to the driver. "You need to stop this bus. I'm getting off."

The driver, paid to do as he was told, pulled off the road and into the dirt, the tires kicking up dust as the bus slowed to a stop. As a final gesture, Laci gave Trent the middle finger and walked off the bus. Maybe Trent hadn't believed her, maybe he thought she was just blowing off steam, because when she actually stepped off the bus, the expression on his face was priceless. And very satisfying. But soon the bus left her behind and she was standing on the side of the road with nothing but her purse and her cell phone and no idea how to get to Woodsville, Kentucky, by four o'clock.

Well, time to put one foot in front of the other and her thumb in the air.

It had been a long time since she'd hitchhiked, but some things were like riding a bike.

She didn't care if she had to walk the entire way. She was getting to that funeral.

CORA ADELLE BRADFORD, born Cora Adelle Johnson, was laid to rest on an unbearably hot fall day surrounded by countless friends and community members she'd touched along her life. In seventy-five years, Cora Bradford had fed whole families, taught Sunday school and shared recipes with more people than any television-chef personality had ever dreamed possible simply by being, at her core, a generous person.

And Kane wasn't ready to say goodbye. Not yet. But even as he struggled with his own grief, it was nothing compared to the heartrending, soul-wrenching grief of the man who'd fallen in love with his country girl at the ripe age of seventeen and she was only fourteen, back when getting married at sixteen wasn't unheard of, if the young man had a good job and solid prospects.

The one saving grace was that Cora wasn't suffering anymore and that's what Kane tried to console himself with, but the small consolation felt hollow against the solid weight of his grief. Rian, wiping his eyes, kept looking toward the back of the chapel, as if waiting for someone to arrive and he couldn't help growling because he knew who his brother was hoping would show up. "She ain't coming," he said. "So stop looking."

"She'll be here. Cora meant the world to her."

"Sure she did."

"Stop it," he whispered tersely. "Don't try measuring the depth of someone else's grief just because you're mad at them."

Great, his little brother, the counselor. "Stop craning your neck to see if Laci is going to show up. We're here for Cora and to say our goodbyes. Besides, Warren needs us right now. I'm worried about the old guy. He's not looking so good."

Rian nodded in agreement. "Is Doc Robbins here? Maybe he could take a look at him, just check him out."

"I don't even know if that old coot is still alive, much less practicing," Kane returned drily. "And besides, there's no way Warren's going to let someone give him a once-over right now. I can barely get him to eat anything since he's returned. I think he's already lost five pounds. His skin is just hanging off him."

"What are we going to do?"

Hell if he knew. The answers weren't falling from the sky and smacking him in the face. "Let's just try and get through this ceremony. One step at a time."

A handful of people said really nice things about Cora and for a woman who'd never had children, she sure touched a lot of lives. It was finally time for Warren to speak and when he shuffled up to the podium he looked a lot older than his seventy-nine years.

His voice, soft and grief-worn, trembled as he slipped his reading glasses over his nose to read what he'd prepared to say.

"Cora said the first time she laid eyes on me, she knew she was going to marry me. I was just a dumb kid, but I was smart enough to know a good thing when I saw it." He paused a beat to collect himself. "She also used to say there's a lid for every pot and we fit together just fine. When I got up the nerve to ask her to marry me, I told her, 'Miss Cora, I ain't a rich man but I'll work hard all of my days to give you a good life if you'll just take a chance on me,' and you know what, she just looked me in the eye and said, 'You hush your mouth. I ain't looking for a soft life or a soft man. I want a man who doesn't lie, works hard and believes in goodness. Are you that man, Warren Bradford?' And I said, 'I hope to be.'" Tears filled Warren's eyes and suddenly the entire church was sniffling, Kane and Rian included. "Cora made me a better man every day. She worked right alongside me to build the ranch, and missing her will be a full-time job. I know you understand what that means because she had this special effect on the people who came into her life. She's leaving behind a giant hole, that's for sure." Warren's gaze drifted to the closed casket and he choked up. "I love you, girl. I love ya."

Warren folded up his paper and tucked it back into his pocket before taking his seat, his eyes glazed with loss. The ceremony concluded and people made the slow exit to the wake, which was held in the adjoining worship hall, and the smell of a dozen different potluck offerings filled the air, but Kane had no appetite. He stayed behind while Rian helped Warren get something to eat, though Kane knew Rian had his work cut out for him. The hard wood beneath his ass began to make his bones ache and he wondered how he was ever going to get back to his life. His business needed him, but Warren needed him, too.

"Did she suffer?"

Kane stiffened at the soft voice at the back of the empty chapel and he didn't need to turn to know that Laci had come, after all. He turned slowly to see Laci standing in the entryway, looking ragged, and nothing like the glamorous country princess that everyone thought they knew.

"No. She passed in her sleep," he answered gruffly, hating how his heart tripled in beat just seeing her there. "You missed the ceremony."

"I caught the important stuff. I heard what Warren said. That was enough for me," she said quietly. "Where is he?"

"With Rian in the worship hall. There's a potluck."

"I'll never understand the custom of feeding people after a death. Seems so morbidly misplaced."

He shrugged without an answer, but he knew she hadn't come to discuss funeral customs. "Why'd you come?"

"What do you mean? That's a hurtful question."

"I tried to call twice. You never called back."

Her face flushed as she explained. "My manager erased the calls. I never got them."

What did it matter? They'd been kidding themselves anyway. It wasn't as if they could build a future together. But there was something about her appearance that made him realize the sincerity in her claim. "How'd you get here?" he asked, noting the slight frazzle in her hair and the fatigue ringing her eyes.

"I got off the tour bus somewhere in Oklahoma, hitchhiked about eight miles to the nearest town, found a small airport and convinced the owner of a private plane to fly me to Kentucky. Then I rented a car from the airport to Woodsville but barely made it in time. All I have are the clothes on my back and whatever is in my purse. Knowing Trent, he probably burned all the stuff I left behind, but I don't care."

"You left your manager?"

"Hell yes, I left him. I realized…" She hesitated a beat, as if she wasn't sure if she'd be able to say what she needed to say. "I realized everything that'd ever mattered was right here…not on a bus. I was trying to get a hold of you, but each time I thought to call, Trent kept me moving at the speed of light and I got sidetracked.

I swear to you, I never got your messages. If I had…I would've been here."

He wasn't going to hold a grudge, not now. Seeing her again, he just wanted to hold on to her. It took everything in him to keep his distance. "Warren will be happy to see you here," he said finally. "You ought to go find him."

She took a bold step toward him, although her gaze was uncertain. "Are you happy to see me?"

That was a loaded question. "It's complicated, Laci, and this isn't the time to figure it out."

Laci nodded. "We'll talk later?"

"Sure," he said, but a part of him didn't know what needed to be said. Their lives weren't compatible. Yet, watching her leave, a hunger that defied reason dogged him and he wanted nothing more than to feel Laci pressed up against him again. Even if it was just to say goodbye for good this time.

But she wanted to talk.

Heart heavy and mind confused, he walked out of the chapel and bypassed the potluck situation. Food wasn't what he wanted.

If he couldn't have Laci in his life, nothing would ever satisfy that particular hunger ever again.

Hell, he had an inkling of the pain Warren was feeling because the idea of accepting that Laci was never going to be his…was like someone slicing his innards with a white-hot knife.

And that sure as hell didn't feel too good.

21

LACI FOUND WARREN with Rian, tucked off in a corner. She approached and Rian met her gaze with a worried one of his own. "Warren?" she ventured, taking a seat beside him. "I'm so sorry… I wanted to be here. I tried so hard to get here. I wish things had ended differently." Warren looked up and smiled with pure love at seeing Laci. She blinked back her own tears as she took in his appearance and asked, "Have you eaten? Looks like plenty of good food out there. I think there was even sweet-potato pie, your favorite."

"No offense to Caroline, but no one makes sweet-potato pie like my Cora. She knew how to put something extra special in the mix," Warren said softly, wiping at his dripping nose with a handkerchief. "She was special, my Cora. So special."

Laci nodded, sharing a worried look with Rian. "That's true. Ain't no one that can make pie like Miss Cora…except *maybe* me. She taught me how to make a few things. Want me to mix something up for you? You look like you haven't had a good meal in days. You're plumb wasting away."

His bottom lip trembled, and after a short beat, he nodded reluctantly. "If it wouldn't be too much trouble. I miss Cora's cooking something fierce. I never realized just how hard it was going to be without her."

"Of course you do," Laci said, nodding as she and Rian helped him to his feet. "You go and let Rian take you home and I'll get what I need to make you something good. I'll only use Miss Cora's recipes, I swear it."

"You're a good girl," he said, lifting a worn, callused hand to caress her jaw. "She loved you, Chickpea. She really did."

Laci covered his hand with hers and blinked back tears. "Thank you, Warren. I loved her, too. Now, you go with Rian and I'll meet you back at the house."

Warren and Rian made their way out of the chapel before too many people swarmed them with condolences and Laci went to find Kane. She found him leaning against his truck, staring up at the dark clouds beginning to crowd the blue skies. He heard her coming and turned to say, "Cora loved these kinds of storms. She said they kept her on her toes, made her feel alive."

Laci chuckled, remembering. "Yeah, because she said she had to run out and get the clothes off the line before they got drenched."

"She was a good woman," he said, choking up. "She took one look at me and made it her mission to fatten me up. I think I put on twenty pounds that first summer."

They could trade stories about Cora all day and night. She was the glue that held together their foundation. There was no replacing a woman like that. But Laci also knew that Cora was a woman who believed in straight talk. She had no patience for beating around the proverbial bush and that's what it felt like she was doing right now, dancing around the elephant in the room. With respect to Cora, Laci decided to just lay it all out there.

"What are we doing?" she asked, shocking him with her quiet yet direct question.

"We're mourning Cora," he said, being deliberately dense. "Let's leave it at that."

She shook her head, not letting it go. "I knew the minute I left that I'd made a mistake," she said, slipping her fingers into his. He curled his fingers around hers almost hesitantly, as if he was afraid to acknowledge that he had feelings he was struggling with, too. "Everything moved so fast I didn't know how to handle it. I slipped back into what felt comfortable, but it wasn't comfortable anymore. Everything felt off. Wrong. I need you, Kane. I need you in my life and I know there are issues…I know it won't be easy, but I'm not a kid anymore and I know what I want." His gaze burned into hers and she knew he was fighting something tooth and nail, so she pressed harder, moving closer, crowding his personal space with her body so that he remembered what it felt like to be naked against one another. "Nothing is impossible if we try. But if we quit on each other…we got no one to blame but ourselves for the misery that we're going to feel. Tell me you didn't miss me," she dared, risking it all—her feelings, her dignity. "Tell me that you didn't want me back."

"Laci…"

She shushed him with a finger against his lips, only to replace it with her mouth. She kissed him sweetly, brushing his lips with hers with the tiniest dart of her tongue against the seam, teasing him with the promise of more. "Tell me, Kane Dalton, that you don't want me."

"I never said I didn't want you. I've always wanted you, Laci."

"Then what are we waiting for?"

"Wanting and having are two separate things." He gently disengaged her grip and stepped away to open his truck door. "This isn't the time or the place to have the discussion you're looking for."

She knew he was right, but she felt they'd lost so much time already and death had a way of clarifying things unlike anything else. "This conversation isn't finished," she told him as he climbed into the truck and started the engine.

"It is for me," he said and pulled away.

She watched the truck drive away and her first impulse was to cry because it felt hopeless, but then she remembered that wearing down Kane Dalton was something she'd figured out how to do when she was fifteen years old. She knew his weaknesses and she wasn't above using them. She didn't know how, but she got the distinct impression Cora was looking down on her, watching and rooting for her with total approval, and that gave her the strength to push forward.

KANE RETURNED TO the ranch and went about his usual chores, but then afterward, took a moment to chat with

Rian about business, which honestly felt like two million miles away in another life.

"You sure you want to talk business?" Rian asked as they went to the cattle enclosure to check a gate that'd been giving Kane trouble. "Business can wait."

"I need something to distract me," he admitted, rubbing at his temple. "Too much going on at the same time, can't think straight."

"Maybe you're overthinking things."

He was too wired up to argue. "Maybe," he admitted. "But humor me. How'd things go with that last gig?"

"Piece of cake. In fact, there was lots of cake. You didn't tell me that at each stop there was going to be some kind of cake with sparklers on it. I swear I gained ten pounds from that gig."

"You didn't have to eat the cake," he reminded his brother, but Rian scoffed at his comment.

"Not eat cake? Are you kidding? There is not a cake I can walk past without getting a little sample. Too many years starving with nothing to eat to walk past something sweet."

Kane could understand that. He still had issues with overbuying food at the grocery store. His place was always well stocked, even if it was just him there. Hell, Laci would get a kick out of everything he had in his pantry... *Stop thinking of Laci*, he told himself, irritated that his mind went there so readily. "Well, you might not have had the most exciting time with Senator Graves, but it's a good way to make the right contacts."

"I'm sure it is. I just prefer my gigs to be a little less

boring. Almost makes me miss an active war zone." He shared a look with Kane. "Almost."

"So what are we going to do about the ranch? We're facing the same issue as we were yesterday."

Rian sighed and lifted his hands with a helpless shrug. "Your guess is as good as mine. I can't even get the man to eat. At this rate, he's going to starve himself in about two weeks."

"Shit," he muttered. "I don't know what to do, either."

"Technically, we're not blood relations, so we have no say in what happens to the ranch and we can't legally help Warren with any kind of money issues that might arise unless he gave one of us power of attorney, and I don't see that happening."

"Yeah, let's not put the cart before the horse," Kane warned. "Cora's just passed and he's struggling, but he'll snap out of it because he loves this place. It's in his blood and he won't let anything happen to it."

"He ought to sell it and move to a retirement place," Rian said, and Kane just stared at his brother as if he'd grown another head.

"Are you crazy? Warren in a retirement home? He'd drive everyone nuts and then get kicked out. No, that's not what's going to happen to Warren. We'll figure something out. Maybe I'll split my time between here and LA." But even as he said it, he knew that wasn't a viable solution, either. He blew out a short breath and then motioned for Rian to help him. "Let's get this gate fixed and then head back before it gets dark."

After securing the gate, they trudged back to the

house and found Laci there, talking to Warren and, miracle of all miracles, she'd managed to fix him a plate of food. She rose from her perch beside Warren and said, "I'm going to start on that pie, but you'd better make a dent in that plate of mashed potatoes or you're gonna hear about it from me. Cora always said it was a crime to waste good food."

"That she did," Warren agreed, lifting his fork with slightly trembling fingers, betraying his low blood sugar. "And Adeline does make a pretty good mash," he said around the bite. "Not as good as my Cora, but pretty good just the same."

Laci caught Kane's grateful expression and she smiled even as she briskly moved around the kitchen in what looked like a mad attempt to make a sweet-potato pie before it was time for bed.

If anyone knew how to reproduce Cora's recipes, it was Laci. Without a daughter to pass on her skills to, Cora had latched onto Laci and found a willing student. Their times in the kitchen had been the way they'd bonded, just as Rian and Kane had bonded with Warren by learning how to care for the animals and the ranch.

It wasn't until later that night, after Laci had put the pie to cool on the counter and Warren had taken himself off to bed, that Kane realized he should've found a hotel to stay in—not because there wasn't room for everyone—but because the temptation of having Laci right there was more than he could possibly deny.

And Laci knew it.

"I'll take the pump house," Rian offered with a yawn,

which nearly prompted Kane to stake his claim on the couch, but Laci had other plans.

Stopping Rian in his tracks with a sweet but firm smile, she said, "You take my old room. Kane and I will take the pump house."

Rian wasn't about to argue. "Yes, ma'am." He tipped an imaginary hat to Laci and offered a quick goodnight, ducking behind a closed door and leaving Kane to fend off Laci all by himself.

She turned to Kane and said, "I told you that conversation wasn't over and I meant it." She slipped her hand into his and said over her shoulder, "Don't think, just move."

He smothered a groan of frustration. There were no more words that needed to be said. Nothing had changed and honestly, things had gotten a lot more complicated now that Cora was gone and they needed solutions, not more problems. But Laci wasn't about to listen to anything that she didn't want to hear, at least not at the moment, and frankly, he was too wrung out to fight her on it.

22

LACI KNEW KANE was resistant and maybe for good reason, but she was done with reason. Reason couldn't explain why her heart tripled in beat when she saw Kane or how her entire body tingled at the mere prospect of feeling his lips on hers. He turned her crank in the best way, and seeing him again had reminded her of how much she'd missed, and all the fame in the world didn't amount to a hill of beans when your heart wasn't full.

"Laci…" He started to survey the small pump house, likely looking for somewhere else to sleep aside from the bed with her, but she was having none of that and immediately started stripping. He stared, his gaze achingly hungry and desperately wanting, even if he was trying to tell a different story with his mouth. "What are you doing?"

"Seems obvious to me. I'm getting naked."

Bless his heart, she thought with a wild rush, he was trying so hard to remain stoic, but soon enough she'd win because there was too much at stake. "You know, the thing about death is that it reminds the living that they've got one life to live. Cora was a vibrant woman and we have to honor the spirit of the woman who told me that a good woman does three things to her man— fills his belly, feeds his soul and satisfies him in bed."

"She said that?" Kane asked, startled.

Laci laughed. "Yes, she did. What the heck do you think we were talking about all those times in the kitchen? Recipes? She was one smart woman. I was just too young to put those lessons into play when it mattered most, but I'm not a kid anymore."

His gaze traveled to her bra and held there as she snapped it open, releasing her breasts, and he sucked in a tight breath. "No, you're not," he agreed, and she knew he itched to reach for her but still he held back. "But this…it's not a good idea."

"Hush." She wiggled out of her panties and tossed them at him. "I'll tell you what's not a good idea… walking away from something real. Cora and Warren were blessed with a true thing, love that doesn't fade with time. I know you feel that way for me because I feel that way about you and I'm not about to let you go without a fight. Not this time." He groaned, fighting himself, but it was only a matter of time. She was on a mission to win and nothing was standing in her way. Especially a button fly. She popped his buttons and pushed his pants down off his hips so she could free his cock. "There it is," she crooned, going to her knees to nuzzle the warm, hard flesh. "Now I'm going to help you shut off that brain of yours."

And then she sucked that lovely cock right down her

throat, gripping his hips and locking her mouth on all that thick, engorged flesh, because Kane was the prize and she played to win.

But soon enough, Kane's groans turned urgent and she knew he was close to coming. He pushed her gently off his cock, and she gasped as he picked her up and tossed her to the bed, covering her with his big, hard body. "You like to play a dangerous game," he told her, the head of his cock pressing against her, insistent, demanding. "I won't be your casual friend with benefits," he warned in a silky voice, even as his hand snaked down to her slick folds and his finger dipped between the dewy flesh. She shuddered when he found her clitoris and teased it with a light but firm touch. "I play for keeps and I don't think you know what that means."

"I want it all," she gasped, clinging to him. "I want you, Kane, and everything that comes with you! I swear. I would s-stop touring—" she held him tightly when he pinched her clitoris, causing her to sweat "—if you wanted me to, I would do anything, Kane. Anything!"

He growled and slid down her body to replace his fingers with his tongue and teeth, lightly nipping the tender, sensitive flesh as he splayed her legs on either side of his face. He ravished that sweet pleasure spot until she was thrashing, crying out, babbling nonsensical words until she came so hard that she went limp, her entire body damp with the sweat popping along her pores. But he was insatiable and ready to split her in two with the force of his thrusts.

It was as if he was possessed with the need to brand her body, because he flipped her over and immediately plunged inside her until she thought for sure he was hitting her tonsils, but it felt so good, so sinfully right, that she arched her back to take more of him. She wanted to be filled with Kane, to be so completely and utterly taken by him that she lost herself to the pleasure of being with the man she'd lost her virginity and heart to so many years ago.

He pounded her, her entire body shaking with each thrust, but she met him with a growl, pushing against him, taking each wonderfully jarring motion with gleeful abandon because she was nearing that beautiful edge, prepared to leap into oblivion. "Yesss, Kane! Yes!" And then she tumbled into sweet bliss as wave after wave of intense pleasure buffeted her body, clenching every muscle and turning her inside out with happy sweetness as Kane followed her with a shout, then withdrew with a shudder to collapse beside her.

Now, that *was how to make a woman forget her own name.* She stared unseeing at the darkened ceiling, drifting on a sea of happiness, knowing that she would settle for nothing less than Kane every night for the rest of her life. She rolled to her side and propped herself onto his chest with a sated smile, saying, "Whatcha thinking about now?"

"Nothing," he admitted with a hoarse, bewildered chuckle. "But then, that was your plan all along, right?"

"Pretty much," she admitted. But as her heart rate slowed to a normal pace and the sweat slowly dried on their bodies, she knew she had to say what needed to be said because while the sex was phenomenal…there was something deeper between them that she wasn't going to let him forget. "I love you, Kane," she said simply, going straight to the point. "I always have and I always will."

"I love you, too," he said, the quiet admission rocking her foundation in the most profound way. "Love isn't and never has been the issue."

Excuse me? She frowned and sat up. "Then what is the problem?"

He tweaked her nipple as he stared up at her. "The problem is that we live different lives."

"I can give up touring," she said, but he shook his head.

"I would never want you to do that. What kind of asshole would I be if I asked that of you?"

"Whatever is in our way, I'll remove it."

"What if it's me?"

Confused, she asked, "What do you mean?"

"What if I'm not cut out to be the man who stands in the shadows while the world gets the best of you? It's selfish and I know it, but I don't want to share and that's just not possible with your career. The thing is, I'm torn. I love that you followed your dreams and achieved wild success because you deserve it. You really do. But I'm afraid that eventually it'll get to me. I don't like the idea of complete strangers whacking off to your picture or plotting to kidnap you. I'd go crazy."

"So your solution is to leave me? What if there is someone out there plotting to kidnap me? What then? Once it happens, *then* you can care?"

He scowled. "That's not what I meant. I already care,

I just…I don't know…Laci…I'm just trying to be honest with you."

"And I'm being honest with you. We'll make it work. People do it all the time. Come with me on tour, be my security detail. No one can protect me more than the man who loves me…the possible father of my children." She let that drop and she watched with happiness as his gaze widened with the idea and she knew it'd been the right thing to say.

"You want kids?" he dared to ask and she nodded. "With me?"

She leaned down to whisper, "I want everything with you," before brushing a kiss across his lips. "I want it all. The house, the kids, the fights, the make-up sex. I'm signing on for the real deal, not the fairy tale. How about you?"

KANE STARED, UNABLE to process the words because his heart was hammering so hard he couldn't breathe. Yes, he wanted it all with Laci. Had always wanted that with Laci, but he'd resigned himself to never having it because their paths were never destined to intersect, but now she was telling him that everything he'd ever wanted could happen if he just had the courage to take that leap of faith with her. He simply couldn't think straight.

"Kane?"

Her questioning gaze brought him back to reality and he shook himself. He needed to stay focused. "And if I said yes…what then? You're in the middle of a tour and I've got a business to run in Los Angeles."

"I'm ready to call it a day with this tour," she said. "Besides, I just fired my manager and I need to find a new one. I'll sell the LA house, keep the Ojai ranch to use as our home base. It's secluded enough and quiet but not totally isolated."

She seemed to have it all figured out and he had to admit, it sounded like a decent plan, but there was Warren to think of now. He sighed and said, "What about Warren? He's falling apart without Cora. We can't leave him alone. I don't even know if he knows how to keep the electric on and the water paid. Cora did all that for him."

Laci considered this for a long moment and then said, "Then we help him. We hire people if we have to."

He shook his head. "Rian and I already thought of that…not gonna happen. He doesn't trust anyone but me and Rian."

"Then we make Woodsville our temporary home," she said resolutely as if that were the easiest solution when he knew it wasn't.

"We can't do that," he protested, but she wasn't interested in arguments and just held her ground. "Okay, and how exactly does that work? We all move in with Warren? I mean, I love the guy, but…"

"No. But we can certainly build our own place on the property. It's plenty big enough," she pointed out, and he realized she was making some sense. Laci settled against him and smiled, saying, "I've always liked that spot across from the barn. The view of the creek is beautiful and the fireflies are magical."

He liked the picture she painted except for one thing. "Have you forgotten how I feel about this town?"

She framed his face with her hands. "This town didn't screw you over. Your father did. And he's dead. Besides, you met me in this town, so it can't be all bad, right?"

She had a point. Still... "I don't know, Laci. There are a lot of variables that I'm not sure will pan out."

"Do you love me?"

"Yes."

"Then that's all that matters," she said, cutting him off softly. "We'll make it work. I need you and you need me. We're like peas and carrots...you know?"

If he were a smart man, he'd just go with whatever she proposed because she was promising the keys to the castle, but he couldn't sell her a bit of goods that he didn't know he could guarantee. "I don't know if I can be the man you want me to be," he said, searching her gaze. "I'm not cut out to be your backstage groupie."

"And I would never ask you to be. But how about being my...husband? Would you be up to that task?"

Her slightly vulnerable gaze seared into his and nearly ripped him to shreds in the best possible way. "Are you saying you want to be my wife?"

"I'm saying we should've been married a long time ago because you're the lid to my pot and if that hasn't been made readily clear, then I don't know what would. What do you say? Want to make an honest woman out of me?"

In answer, he crushed her to him, sealing his lips to hers and she clung to him like a monkey. Suddenly he lost his grip on every objection he'd raised in earnest because she was the only woman for him. He would never tire of this feeling and he knew that with Laci, this feeling would never stop. They had something people only dreamed about, something few people were lucky enough to find and hold on to. The same something Cora and Warren had been blessed to have and then teach their ragtag pseudofamily how to know when they saw it.

And he'd be a damn idiot to let it go twice.

"Damn straight I will marry you, Laci McCall. Hell, maybe we'd better do it quick before either one of us comes to their senses and realizes it's a terrible idea."

"Hush your mouth," she said, giggling in his arms. "It's the best damn idea you've ever had. Now get over here and show me how much you love me."

"Yes, ma'am." And then he gladly, almost deliriously, showed her just how being her husband would become his number one priority for the rest of their days.

Making it work wouldn't be easy, but…hell, nothing worth keeping ever was.

Epilogue

A LOT CAN happen in a year.

Kane stood with Laci as they prepared to walk over the threshold of their new home, built to their particular specifications on the Bradford ranch, and grinned. "Not bad," he said, and Laci batted him playfully on the arm. "Okay, okay, it's pretty damn awesome," he admitted, looking at the modest three-bedroom, two-bath replica farmhouse that'd originally been on the property back in the 1800s. They'd found the picture when they were going back in the records to handle a land dispute that'd popped up and the minute Laci had seen it, she'd known that was the house she wanted built on the property. Of course, Warren, tickled pink to have his family close again, was quick to agree with her and before Kane knew it, they were knee-deep in construction and historical documents to make sure every detail was just right.

It was then he realized his new wife was a little obsessive.

But lucky for him, he found that little hidden quality damn hot.

"Who knew picking out door handles could be so sexy," he teased, and she blushed.

"They have to be right or else it throws off the entire historical relevance," she insisted. "And if we'd gone with the brushed bronze, it would've clashed with the copper I'd already picked out for the appliances. So I had to find a way to get you to see my way was right."

"It worked," he said, smiling. "We should build more houses together. The sex is fantastic."

"Yoooo-hoooo," a voice called out from behind them and they turned to see Adeline Verley making her way toward them, holding a pie. "You can't go into your new house without something sweet to start you off on a good note."

About three months after Cora had passed, Adeline, who'd been bridge buddies with Cora, started coming around to check on Warren. And as things go, Warren started to like more about Adeline than just her creamy mashed potatoes. Rian, Kane and Laci wholeheartedly approved of this new "friendship" and actively encouraged it because Adeline was a lot like Cora, which Warren found comforting, and the fact that she could bake as well as his late wife was a big point in her favor. Even though no one would ever replace Cora, Adeline was a good woman and they all agreed, Cora would've approved.

"Smells great, Adeline," Laci said, accepting the pie with a smile. "Rhubarb?"

"Straight from my own garden." She beamed, then

exclaimed, "Oh, my word! That house…just beautiful. When y'all gonna start filling up those rooms with
some babies?"

Laci laughed and Kane shifted on his feet, but Adeline wasn't kidding. Babies might be in their future
someday, but right now, Kane was having too much fun
making his wife squeal every night, screwing her six
ways from Sunday because…as Laci put it, they had a
lot of catching up to do.

And boy, he liked the work.

Rian kept the LA office going and Laci had kept her
Ojai ranch for times when trips to SoCal were unavoid-
able, but for the most part, they were ready to make
Woodsville their primary location and Kane was good
with that. So much had happened, so much had changed
and he realized if he wasn't the same person from all
those years ago, the town wasn't the same, either.

Second chances were available to those willing to
accept them.

And Kane was ready.

"Oh, by the way, another fat restitution check came
in today, so that should more than pay for the landscap-
ing I want to put in," Laci told him, smiling angelically.
"See? I'm being frugal."

He laughed at the very idea of his wife being frugal
in any way, but he figured it was money well spent.
After an audit had been performed on Trent Blackstone,
it was discovered he'd been ripping Laci off from the
minute she'd hit it big and he owed her a lot of money.
A judge had ordered restitution, which had pretty much
wiped out Trent's bank accounts and now he was no

longer in the business. Rumor had it, he'd switched to the insurance field. Laci said she didn't care—that she never thought of Trent—but she sure loved cashing those checks.

As for her tour team, Audrey and Simone were still her go-to people and while Laci hadn't managed to convince either to move to Woodsville because, c'mon, it's barely a blip on the map and hardly a mecca for upwardly mobile professionals, Laci saw them often because they were staying at the Ojai ranch to keep it occupied and free from squatters.

Hey, life was good. Laci had a new hit single, a song that had been stuck in her head for close to two years and now was climbing the charts like a money-hungry gold digger and he had the sexiest wife who could bake a mean pie during the day and ride him senseless at night.

What more could a guy want when he had the hottest ticket in town?

Not much.

And he was good with that.

So, so good.

* * * * *

Be sure to look for Kimberly Van Meter's
next Harlequin Blaze,
SEX, LIES AND DESIGNER SHOES,
in August 2015!

COMING NEXT MONTH FROM

REQUEST YOUR FREE BOOKS!
2 FREE NOVELS PLUS 2 FREE GIFTS!

H HARLEQUIN®

Blaze

red-hot reads!

YES! Please send me 2 FREE Harlequin® Blaze® novels and my 2 FREE gifts (gifts are worth about $10). After receiving them, if I don't wish to receive any more books, I can return the shipping statement marked "cancel." If I don't cancel, I will receive 4 brand-new novels every month and be billed just $4.74 per book in the U.S. or $5.21 per book in Canada. That's a savings of at least 14% off the cover price. It's quite a bargain. Shipping and handling is just 50¢ per book in the U.S. and 75¢ per book in Canada.* I understand that accepting the 2 free books and gifts places me under no obligation to buy anything. I can always return a shipment and cancel at any time. Even if I never buy another book, the two free books and gifts are mine to keep forever.

150/350 HDN GH2D

Name	(PLEASE PRINT)

Address	Apt. #

City	State/Prov.	Zip/Postal Code

Signature (if under 18, a parent or guardian must sign)

Mail to the **Reader Service:**
IN U.S.A.: P.O. Box 1867, Buffalo, NY 14240-1867
IN CANADA: P.O. Box 609, Fort Erie, Ontario L2A 5X3

Want to try two free books from another line?
Call 1-800-873-8635 or visit www.ReaderService.com.

* Terms and prices subject to change without notice. Prices do not include applicable taxes. Sales tax applicable in N.Y. Canadian residents will be charged applicable taxes. Offer not valid in Quebec. This offer is limited to one order per household. Not valid for current subscribers to Harlequin Blaze books. All orders subject to credit approval. Credit or debit balances in a customer's account(s) may be offset by any other outstanding balance owed by or to the customer. Please allow 4 to 6 weeks for delivery. Offer available while quantities last.

Your Privacy—The Reader Service is committed to protecting your privacy. Our Privacy Policy is available online at www.ReaderService.com or upon request from the Reader Service.

We make a portion of our mailing list available to reputable third parties that offer products we believe may interest you. If you prefer that we not exchange your name with third parties, or if you wish to clarify or modify your communication preferences, please visit us at www.ReaderService.com/consumerchoice or write to us at Reader Service Preference Service, P.O. Box 9062, Buffalo, NY 14240-9062. Include your complete name and address.

HBI5

SPECIAL EXCERPT FROM

H HARLEQUIN®

Blaze

*After years away, Cade Gallagher rushes back to
Thunder Mountain Ranch when he learns his foster
mom is in the hospital. But returning means facing his
past, and the woman he left behind…*

Read on for a sneak preview of
MIDNIGHT THUNDER,
the first book in
Vicki Lewis Thompson's
sexy new cowboy saga
THUNDER MOUNTAIN BROTHERHOOD.

"Thanks. This is great." Cade led Hematite into the stall,
unhooked the lead rope and rubbed the horse's neck.
"You're safe now, buddy. I'll be back to check on you in
a few hours."

Hematite bumped his nose against Cade's arm. Then
he walked over to the hay rack and began to munch.

Cade let out a breath as he left the stall and latched it
behind him. While he coiled the lead rope, he gazed at the
horse. "If I didn't know better, I'd think he understood
what I just told him. I've never seen him so relaxed."

"At the very least, he probably picked up on your
relief."

"I *am* relieved. I had no idea if this would work, if I
could transport him from hell to heaven." He glanced at
Lexi. "Thanks for making it possible."

She shrugged. "Don't thank me. I'm only doing what

Herb and Rosie would want."

He repositioned his hat in a typical Cade gesture. "They love to be of service, thank God. If they hadn't come along…"

Her heart squeezed. "I know."

"Yes, you do." He held her gaze. "You know that more than anyone. Lexi, I—"

"Go see Rosie." She wasn't ready for a heart-to-heart. "We're both tired. We'll talk later."

He nodded. "All right. But let me say this much. I've missed you every single day."

She swallowed her instinctive response. She'd missed him every single day, too, but she wasn't going to admit it. "Go see Rosie."

He turned as if to walk out of the barn. Then he swung back and reached for her. Before she could protest he'd pulled her into his arms and brought his mouth down on hers. It was a hard kiss, a kiss filled with frustration. There was no tenderness, only heat and confusion. It was over before she could respond.

He left the barn without looking back. Heart pounding, she pressed her fingers to her mouth. She still loved him with every fiber of her being. And he still loved her. But as she'd learned five years ago, love wasn't enough.

Don't miss
MIDNIGHT THUNDER by Vicki Lewis Thompson,
available in June 2015 wherever
Harlequin® Blaze® books and ebooks are sold.

Love the Harlequin book you just read?

Your opinion matters.

Review this book on your favorite book site, review site, blog or your own social media properties and share your opinion with other readers!

JUST CAN'T GET ENOUGH?

Join our social communities
and talk to us online.

You will have access to the latest
news on upcoming titles and special
promotions, but most importantly,
you can talk to other fans about your
favorite Harlequin reads.

Harlequin.com/Community

Facebook.com/HarlequinBooks

Twitter.com/HarlequinBooks

Pinterest.com/HarlequinBooks

THE WORLD IS BETTER WITH

Romance

Harlequin has everything from contemporary, passionate and heartwarming to suspenseful and inspirational stories.

**Whatever your mood,
we have a romance just for you!**

Connect with us to find your next great read, special offers and more.

f /HarlequinBooks

y @HarlequinBooks

www.HarlequinBlog.com

www.Harlequin.com/Newsletters

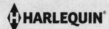

◆ HARLEQUIN®

A *Romance* FOR EVERY MOOD™

www.Harlequin.com